MOWING AND BLOWING

Gay Sex in the Garden

PETER SCHUTES   CHUCK IDGAF   J. W. STEED

Contents

THE CITY GARDENER
BY PETER SCHUTES

My name is Pedro, but my friends call me Pete. I'm a city gardener in San Francisco, the land of fruits and nuts. I used to work in Golden Gate Park, but my drinking got me into trouble, so they gave me the shittiest, loneliest assignment: Collingwood Park. That's the park in the Castro where the queers do their dirty business at night. It's just a big baseball field, really. It would be an easy job if it weren't for all the needles, dirty ass wipes, beer cans, and those weird little broken glass vials I have to pick up. Every morning at dawn, I chase away the speed freaks and sex junkies so I can clean up their mess. I water the plants at the Rec Center, and once a week, I drive the mower around the baseball diamond to keep the grass at bay.

Fags. I'm kind of jealous of how much sex they have. My old lady left me 'cause of all the drinking. That and because my dick was too big. Bitch. These days, it's just mother-fist and her five fingers. I wish there was a park where women gave it out for free. Oh, sure, I can pay a hundred bucks down on Capp Street, but that'd leave me broke with a case of the clap. No, I don't get any.

Heating Up

❦

That was my attitude when my story started. I'm different now. Here's what happened.

It was a typical cold August morning. While the rest of the bay was cooking in the summer heat, San Francisco was sweater weather. It was another Saturday - time to trim the baseball field before the gay softball league had their game. I got to work a little late, so I was behind. My morning beer demanded a whiskey chaser. I bundled up against the fog, filled my flask, and hopped on the 33 to take me to the Castro. If I didn't have that morning drink, I'd be shaking by the afternoon. That's how bad it was, but I didn't think there was anything wrong with it. I used to say, "I don't got a drinking problem. I drink. I get drunk. No problem!"

It was a good thing I didn't like drugs, or I'd be dead by now.

The city gardeners that got into coke, speed, or smack were all washed up. I lost a couple of friends to drugs. I thought I was better than them because I didn't break the law by drinking.

By the time I got to Collingwood, the fog had burnt off. I was too drunk to notice how hot it was. Then the fucking tractor mower up and quit on me. I was gonna

5

have to use a small gas mower instead, and I was behind schedule. I took a big hit off my flask and pulled the starter cable until the mower leaped into life. I didn't have time to fuck with cleaning up condoms and shit, so I just started mowing.

I started to feel lightheaded and thought maybe I needed another drink. I drained the flask, thinking it would set me right. It didn't. I started to see fog around the edges of my vision, and it kept getting foggier until I was looking out a small hole. Then it turned red and the lights went out.

I woke up in Davies Hospital. I sat up and called for a nurse. That's when I saw him. The guy in the chair next to me was a big muscle fag, uh, gay guy. He stood up.

"I'll get you a nurse. Just sit tight."

I was flustered. *Who was this guy?*

He brought a nurse back to my room.

"Glad to see you're awake." The nurse checked my pulse. The muscle dude sat back in his chair.

I leaned into the nurse and asked her, "Who's this guy?" I gestured towards the muscle guy.

"It's Greg, your lover. You don't remember him? I think we might need a doctor."

The guy, Greg, stood up. "Pedro's just a little confused. Can you give me a minute alone with him?"

The nurse sighed and left the room.

I glowered at the guy. "What gives?"

He shushed me. "Keep it down. I'll explain."

I didn't feel too good just then and lay back down, waiting for the room to stop spinning.

He continued. "I told them you were my lover, so the ambulance would take you. They said if he was just another drunk passed out in the park, there was no need to bring you in."

"How do you know my name?"

Greg shrugged. "I fished in your wallet for your insurance card. It was kinda obvious."

”What happened to me? I gotta get back to work.”

I sat up, but Greg gently pushed me back down in the bed.

”It was a combination of the booze, the hard work, and your warm clothes. It's a heat wave out there. Didn't you notice? Or were you too drunk?”

I took offense. “Fuck you, man. I wasn't drunk!”

”Your breath tells me otherwise. Look, I gotta get to work at the bookstore. You're lucky I found you.”

He was right. But I was an asshole. “You didn't try any faggy shit with me when I was passed out, did you?”

”I'm going to pretend you didn't just say that, Pedro. I saw a fellow alcoholic in need, and I helped him. It's what we do in the program.”

”Program? You don't look like an alcoholic.”

Greg smiled. “Believe me, I was a gutter drunk. Passed out drunk too many times to remember.”

I was still offended. ”I ain't no alcoholic, neither. You one of those AA'ers I hear about?”

Greg nodded. “Like I said, I gotta get back to work. You take care, Pedro.” He winked and left the room. I watched his ass jiggle when he walked. It felt confusing. Why did I care what his ass looked like?

The nurse came back in. “You still don't remember your lover?”

I thought about it. My instinct would have been to say I wasn't queer, but Greg had done me a solid. Plus, I didn't want no doctor looking at me. So I said, “I remember. I was just disoriented or whatever.”

She smiled. She was an old lady. Still, I'd have fucked her if she was up for it. Nurses turn me on. But I'd probably tear a hole in that old pussy. I'm not kidding. My dick is just way too big. I hide it in my loose coveralls when I'm at work, but the guys all know. I miss the other gardeners. Like I said, Collingwood is a lonely place. But I don't miss them calling me "Big Peter" or "Pedro Pollón." They think they'd have it better if they was like me, but they don't know. I get turned down regularly. My old lady gave it her best, but like I said, between the alcohol and painful sex, she didn't want me. That hurt. Not everybody wishes they had a bigger dick.

Davies Hospital wanted to keep me there. They were going to transfer me to UCSF to a locked ward. My city insurance was like a gold mine for those greedy doctors. But I talked my way out of it. They told me I needed to go to AA. Ha! That was the second time that day I heard about it.

I sweet-talked them until they were about to let me go, when the DTs kicked in. I had a seizure, and woke up on a gurney. They rushed me to an ambulance and before I knew it, I was at the Drug and Alcohol ward at UCSF. Fuck, they were a bunch of sickos in there. So that's Part One of my story.

Hot Blooded

Yeah, that was it. I was stuck in a locked ward where they even gave me little shots of alcohol every few hours to keep me from seizing up for a day or two. I kept asking about my job, but they promised me it would be waiting for me when I got better.

Better. I certainly wasn't doing too well. I could have done with some improvements. So I settled into it. What the fuck, right? Free food, no work, and maybe even a better life at the end of it all. My liver, they said, was fatty and getting cirrhosis. If I didn't quit, well, I'd die from it.

Every Thursday night, they had an optional "jails and institutions" AA meeting. Some sap would come and talk to us about their miserable life and then how it turned around. They called it experience, strength, and hope. I thought it was a bunch of bullshit, but the cookies and coffee were good, so I stayed. I didn't hear anything that moved me.

I shared a room with three other guys. It seemed like every time I was in there, someone else was there, too. I needed to get off real bad. My balls hurt. But jacking off would be a big production number; I couldn't just tug one out like a normal guy. The bathroom might work, but it was two stalls and a urinal, and it didn't lock. Plus, it was always busy. I was going nuts.

That's when this queen approached me. He went by Denise, but the nurses all called him Dennis. He wore his hospital gown like a mini-skirt, with an improvised belt that made it look feminine. Like me, he didn't have anybody to bring him new clothes, and mine had gotten lost somewhere between Davies and the ambulance ride, so all either of us got was hospital gowns.

My family's Spanish from way back, like Mission Dolores way back. But since the nurses all called me Pedro, Dennis says to me, "You are one pale Mexican."

I shrugged. "I ain't Mexican. I'm Spanish."

"Spanish, Mexican, it's the same, isn't it? A hot-blooded Latino."

I felt my blood boil, but I kept my cool. I didn't need no trouble on the ward. Then Dennis puts his hand on my crotch and jumps back, startled. "Damn, Pedro, that's a big one."

I was so hard up for sex I couldn't stop it. I started getting a boner. I turned red.

"Come with me." Because Dennis was gay, they gave him his own room away from the other guys. He pulled me into the room and shut the door, and lights off.

If I squinted my eyes, Dennis looked like a Denise. He kept his face shaved. I was desperate enough that I let that faggot - that guy jack me off. To his credit, he was pretty talented. My old lady didn't have a dick and didn't know what a guy wants out of a hand job. Denise knew. He knelt down and put the tip in his mouth. That was about all he could manage.

"Oh, Pedro, you're huge. Oh, god, it's so beautiful."

No one ever called my dick beautiful before; big, scary, gate crasher, hole wrecker but never had anyone said it was beautiful. I closed my eyes and pretended he was a woman. I even half opened them and he still looked like a woman with his long, bleached hair. I ran my hands through the hair, surprised at how it didn't make any difference if he was a guy or not. I needed to come, and Denise was gonna get me there.

He held my dick in both hands, taking long, fast strokes while he slurped on the end. I had to admit it was the best blow job I'd ever had. Then he surprised me. He opened his mouth really wide and took another couple of inches. I felt my dick rub the back of his throat. Nobody had ever done that before. It was too much.

"Dude, I'm gonna come."

Denise nodded. His mouth was full.

"I mean it, Denise, I'm gonna come in your mouth.

"Mmmhmm." He wanted it. Gross.

I started breathing fast, and my balls lifted up against my dick. Then I came so hard it squirted past Denise's lips, spraying my hospital gown with goop. Denise swallowed down as much as she could. Or he. I don't know what he was. But he could suck my big dick better than anyone.

He wiped his mouth and kissed my cheek. I pushed him away.

"Don't do that!"

Denise said, "I just sucked your cock; I think a peck on the cheek is the least you can let me have."

"You got cum on my face."

"Sorry, sweetie." Denise lifted his gown and wiped my face. It was weird how queens could make a guy feel cared for. But that's how I felt just then. It was embarrassing. Then he pushed me out of his room and closed the door.

That was the first time I ever did anything gay. It wasn't as bad as I thought. No lightning bolt came down from heaven and struck me dead. None of the nurses knew or cared that it happened. It just was. My head and my heart went sideways, fighting each other like two brothers trying to get the last cookie out of the jar. I wanted a drink so badly, but I was dry and had to stay that way. Maybe I could get a PRN of Valium or something.

I didn't realize I was crying when I approached Nurse Cecilia.

"I gotta bad case of the shakes. Can you give me something?"

She shook her head. "I'm sorry, Pedro, it's been more than a week. We have to keep you off all substances now to give your liver a rest."

I wish to God I'd stuffed some drugs under my mattress. I was in emotional agony. What the fuck did I just do? Was I a faggot now?

Cecilia saw my tears. "Do you need to talk to someone? I can get you a counselor."

I was so ashamed and embarrassed I could feel my skin turn red.

"I can't. I can't talk about it."

She put an arm around my shoulder and led me to the counselor's office. He was at lunch. I cried like a stupid baby. I sat in the counselor's office for 10 minutes until he came in. He was a round man with a kind face. I'd never been to counseling.

"Pedro? I'm David." We shook hands.

"It's Pete." I grabbed a tissue from his desk and blew my nose.

"Pete. Got it. What's going on, Pete?"

I shook my head while another wave of tears flooded over me. I felt like a bitch. I mean, I don't think I cried since my dad beat it out of me 20 years ago. What the fuck was wrong?

"We can just sit here, Pete. I don't need you to tell me anything until you're ready."

I wanted to get up and leave, but the truth was burning a hole in my stomach.

"I'm ready. I think. Can you promise me what I say won't leave this room?"

David said, "If you're planning to kill someone or

yourself, I have to tell someone else. Otherwise, anything you say here stays here."

I wasn't sure I believed him. Nobody could find out. *But fuck it, right?*

"I, uh, I let another guy suck my dick."

David nodded. "And?"

I stared at him. He didn't seem the least bit upset. "And I'm not a fag, and it's wrong!"

David smiled. "Pete, relax. Whatever your parents or your friends told you about sex is probably wrong. Let's unpack this. What thoughts are running through your head right now?"

I said, "I'm not a fag. I'm not. I just let a guy suck my dick."

"Did you enjoy it?"

I got mad. "What kind of faggot question is that? Did I enjoy it?"

David shrugged. "Did you?"

"Um, yeah. Sorta."

David patted my hand. "Pete, it's okay to do stuff that feels good. Sex feels good. All kinds of sex, not just the kind you're used to."

"Getting drunk feels good, too, but I can't do that anymore, right?"

David said, "Yeah. And if you have too much sex, you'll probably find out the same thing. But I'm guessing you don't have too much sex despite your good looks."

He was pissing me off. "What makes you say that? I get plenty."

He shrugged. "It's my job to figure out what's going on with people and help them. I don't know why I know it, but I do. You've pushed a lot of people away with your drinking; that's pretty obvious. But something else keeps women away. I don't know what it is; I just sense it."

He knew my whole hand, and we'd only just met. It

was weird. It felt like a relief to start admitting this shit, too.

"Yeah, I got a problem. A big problem." I grabbed my crotch through the hospital gown and shook my dick. "It's too much."

David kept his cool. "Judging by the size, I'd say it probably is too much for a lot of women. Maybe you just haven't met the right one yet."

"Haven't met the right one yet? Fuck those bitches."

David didn't judge me. He didn't say anything. He let long silences fill the room, and I just kept going.

"I mean, fuck. All the guys think I got it made because I've got a huge pecker, but they don't know. They don't. They think I can have all the pussy I want. But I can't. Women think they want it until it's time to get down to business. Then they chicken out. Say mean shit."

When David said nothing, I went on.

"And then this dude, he was like so appreciative, you know? I mean, he did it right. He blew me like he really wanted to. No bitch is ever gonna do that."

David said, "Do you want him to do it again?"

"Hell yeah. But that means I'm a fag."

David cleared his throat. "You are aware that 'fag' is a rude word. You're letting an ugly word describe something beautiful inside you. Your sexuality is a gift. It's not a slur. You're as straight or gay as you want to be. You choose not society, not some ugly word, not your parents, not your friends."

I felt something heavy lifted off my shoulders. Like I was taking off my protective gear after a football game. It was a relief. I cried some more. David handed me another tissue. I took it gratefully and blew my nose.

"Pete, I'm glad we had this talk. This is the kind of stuff that sends a man back out to drink if he doesn't talk about it. Have you been to the AA meeting?"

I nodded. "This..this is like the Fourth Step, yeah?"

David nodded. "Secrets and shame are deadly diseases for alcoholics like us."

"Wait, you're an alcoholic?"

David chuckled. "And a junky, too. You look so surprised. I was forced into the program through jail. It saved my life. Now I give it back."

I was surprised. He was so together, like REALLY together. Like you'd never know he'd done anything bad his whole life. It was inspiring. It made me want to be a better person.

Denise Opens the Door

T hursday night was a shocker. I get to the meeting a little late, and the speaker is Greg, the guy who scraped me off the playing field and got me to Davies Hospital. He saw me walk in, and his eyes lit up.

The whole meeting, I sat there embarrassed, waiting for him to point at me and tell my story. But he didn't. He was cool, and so was his story. I can't really tell it because of the anonymity thing and all. So I'll just say he drank me under the table. My story was nothing so bad as his.

When the meeting was over, I rushed the cookies and coffee, hoping to sneak off before Greg could talk to me. But I felt his hand land on my shoulder.

"Pete. You don't know how glad I am to see you at a meeting."

I felt those damn emotions again. I held back tears as best I could when I said, "Thank you for saving me the other day."

Greg said, "You don't have to thank me. Just return the favor for someone else someday. Who knows? It might even be me that you save!"

I said, "You? But you're cured."

He laughed long and hard. When his chuckles subsided, he said, "There is no cure. This is the best thing we got. A daily reprieve from drinking. We put one day next to another, but nothing we do ourselves can stop us from drinking. That's God's job."

I felt the same way about God that I felt about Santa Claus and the Tooth Fairy. It didn't make sense when he said it. My face must have shown it.

Greg said, "Don't worry, just keep coming to these meetings and it will start to make sense. Call me if you need a ride to a good meeting after you get out." He handed me a business card that was just his name and a phone number. Keep it tight, and follow the light."

Greg turned to leave, and I caught myself looking at his ass in those tight polyester slacks. I looked away, but instead of shame, I felt a little bit of lust creep in. I guess Dave's talk had opened the floodgates. I didn't know I felt like this until I got head from Denise. Stuff changed inside that day, and it was a good thing.

Right after the meeting, I found Denise smoking and watching TV in the common area.

"Pete! How are you, honey?" He patted his hand on the sofa for me to sit down.

I shook my head. "It's uh. Can we do that thing again?"

Denise leaped off the sofa. He waved his arm towards his room. "Right this way, monsieur."

I was still in there for two more weeks. I kept Denise busy two or three times a day. He was good. It was like sex had been nothing but a joke before that. This was serious. It blew my mind how he didn't want nothing in return. It was like me fucking his face was all he needed. He didn't want to get off with me there. It was like we both gave the other exactly what they wanted. I still get hard thinking about those blowjobs. Denise did his damnedest to take my cock in his throat, but it only went into the tip and no further. He said it was because they never took his tonsils out. He promised me there were cocksuckers who could take the whole thing. I didn't care because it felt good just like it was. Every time I shot a load in Denise's mouth, I heard him moan with pleasure like I'd just made his mouth come. Dicks are ugly to me. Denise didn't want me to see his dick, and it was good. The whole thing was just what I needed. Maybe God did exist, and this was his way of proving it.

I didn't think anyone knew what was going on between me and Denise. More importantly, I didn't care if anyone knew. I was ready to beat the first man who said anything bad about Denise. He was a gentle kind of guy, sensitive, and I felt protective of him. Not like he was my bitch or anything. He was just someone who probably couldn't defend himself and who also probably got a lot of shit for being the way he was.

One day, in the common room, A fat, bald guy named Arnie called Denise out for staring at him.

He said, "Denise, you're one ugly motherfucker. Don't look at me, you fuckin' queer."

Before I knew it, I was on my feet with my hand around Arnie's neck, fist raised, ready to punch his lights out. Then I thought about where I was and what would happen if I got violent. So I let go of Arnie's neck and lowered my fist.

"Don't talk to him like that. Show some respect."

Arnie spat on the ground. "Respect? That faggot deserves respect?"

I wanted to knock him senseless, but I kept cool. "Every one of us is in here for the same fuckin' thing, Arnie. We all need respect. Even a piece of shit like you."

Denise laughed behind me. Then Arnie laughed. It was like I had done something good in my life for once. I laughed, too. After that, nobody fucked with Denise.

On my 29th day, the day before the insurance would run out and I'd have to go back to my life, I took Denise aside and shut the door to his room.

"Look, Denise. I don't want to hurt you. This is our last day together."

Denise shrugged. "You can't hurt me, Pete. I'm not looking for love."

It hurt when I heard that. I realize now that it was because I was looking for love and didn't want to admit it. But at that moment, it just felt like a bittersweet relief.

Denise said, "Now, let me have another go." He knelt down, lifting my cock head to his velvet lips, swallowing as fast as he could before it got too big. He managed almost six inches this last time. But then I got fully hard, and he had to pull back. It was fine. I'd never been all the way inside a woman. I'd bottom out at about eight inches and left the rest exposed. That's just how it was. What mattered was Denise's tongue and lips, his hands holding and stroking me, cupping my balls, milking them like a cow. I grunted like a pig; it felt so fucking good.

When we were done, Denise gestured for me to wait while he brushed his teeth. Then he wrapped his arms around my neck and gave me a deep-tongued kiss. My base instinct was to push him away, but I let it pass and enjoyed the kiss. I even got half hard under my gown. Denise felt me brush his thigh.

"Ready for another?"

I nodded. I was ready.

Crash Pad

❦

Wearing some donated clothes, they only give you when you leave, I must have looked like a bum. The wool pants were too tight in the crotch, showing every inch of my cock trapped against my right thigh and my big balls squashed against the left. The T-shirt was too big. The shoes were scuffed and faded. I had a cab voucher, so I took it back to my pad in the Richmond, only to remember that my keys were lost along with my clothes. My landlord, Edsel Chow, lived across the park in the Sunset. I didn't know what to do. I fished in my ugly, tight pants and found Greg's card. He said he'd give me a ride to a meeting, so maybe he'd give me a ride to Edsel's place. I felt like a criminal calling him collect.

"Collect call from Pete from the Park. Will you accept the charges?"

Greg said, "Yes, of course I will."

I said, "Hey, Greg. I got out, and I don't have my fucking...don't have my keys. Do you think I could get a ride to my landlord's house?"

Greg showed up in five minutes in a cream-colored Mercedes rag top. I stared at it in shock. I knew he had his shit together, but I didn't realize it was Mercedes-Benz together. *I thought he worked at a bookstore. How does a guy working at a bookstore get that kind of scratch?*

"Get in!"

I smiled and hopped over the door, landing in the passenger seat with a thud. He drove a little recklessly through Golden Gate Park until we got to the outer Sunset, where it was 20 degrees colder and packed with dense fog.

We pulled up to Edsel's place.

"I'll be right back, hopefully."

Greg waved his hand. "Take your time. I'm not busy today."

I wondered what he did that meant he could "not be busy" on a weekday. Who knows how rich people stay rich?

My face was the color of cigarette ash when I came back to the car.

"Pete? Are you okay?"

I shook my head. "The fucker threw out all my stuff and rented the place to someone else."

"You still have your job, though, right?"

I shrugged. "They said I would."

Greg said, "Let's go back to mine. You can stay in my guest room tonight unless you're planning on drinking."

I had to admit, this fucked up situation made a bottle of booze sound pretty tempting.

I said, "I want to get drunk. So let's see if God can stop me."

Greg beamed. "Good answer."

We raced through the Presidio and up Russian Hill. He turned into the driveway of a mansion.

"Can you get the garage door?"

I looked up at the house. "That's your place?"

He laughed. "No, I live in the old servant's quarters. I wish that was my place."

I had a lot of questions, but they were probably rude, so I just followed him to the back of the property, to a little house.

The living room had a giant picture window with a

view of the Financial District, Telegraph Hill, and the Bay. There was only one bedroom, a kitchen, and a bathroom. I didn't see a guest room.

Greg said, "I have a spare room downstairs. It's just a room. There's no bathroom or anything. I hope that's okay."

I said, "It's a lot better than what I got right now."

Greg said, "Can I get you some water, maybe a glass of juice?"

I said, "No, thanks. Oh, unless you got a Coke?"

He grinned and pulled out a bottle of Coke from his fridge. "Have a Coke and a smile!"

After four weeks of hospital orange juice and coffee, that Coca-Cola tasted like it came from God's faucet.

After I finished my Coke, I rang up work and confirmed I'd start the following Monday.

Greg said, "If you want to stay here until your next paycheck, you can."

I said, "I got a few bucks in the bank. Oh, but shit, how am I going to get money out? That asshole threw out everything. My passbook, my birth certificate, all of it's gone."

Greg said, "The longest journey begins with a single step. Why don't we write down all the stuff you need before you start work on Monday? Let me get a pad and pen."

Why was Greg being so nice to me? What did he want? I looked down at my cock, bulging along the seams of my pants, and thought maybe that was what he wanted.

I knew I would be a jerk if I asked, so I did it anyway. "Do...do you want something from me?"

Greg stopped whistling and put down the pad of paper he'd found in a drawer. "What do you mean, Pete? Rent? No. Don't be silly!"

I looked down at my dick bulging in my pants. Greg got my silent message. He frowned.

"I won't lie. I felt that cock in your pants when I got

your wallet out. I would be lying if I said I didn't think about it. I'm human and gay."

I waited, like I'd seen David do. It worked.

"You don't swing that way anyway, Pete. Don't start something. I'm trying to help you out."

I was sure he'd say something different, not turn me down like that. I said, "So you don't want this?" I grabbed and shook my cock.

Greg sat down. "Look, Pete. I don't know what you want, but what you need at this moment is to stay focused so we can get you back on your feet again. You landed hard out of the hospital, and I'd like to help you get up."

I said, "I heard 'hard' and 'help you get up'."

"Stop it!" Greg was smiling when he said it.

"I'm just fucking with you."

Greg said, "I heard 'fucking with you.'"

And that was it. I grabbed Greg and pulled him close. I felt his breath grow hot against my face before he tilted his head and closed his eyes, welcoming my lips to his. I grabbed his ass, surprised by how hard it was. Not like a girl's ass. But he relaxed it, and it jiggled in my hands.

Then he pulled back. "Stop! We can't do this. You're 30 days sober."

His breath came in deep pants.

I said, "I know you want me."

Greg said, "I want you sober, is what I want. So let's stop all this and work on your mess."

The hospital had unlocked my sex life. I didn't care if Greg was a boy or a girl. I needed a blow job right then. But he seemed to think it was a bad idea. Even gay guys got hang-ups.

I made a list of all the shit I needed to get done. I needed to get my birth certificate so I could get my driver's license so I could get my money out of the bank. Fuck! It was a lot of stuff. Drinking myself to an early grave seemed easier than being sober doing all this crap. At least Greg offered to drive me around the next day.

Greg had some pants that fit me loosely, which was a relief. He gave me a clean t-shirt that fit better than the crap from the hospital and a nice Derby jacket with the gold paisley lining. His feet were a lot smaller than mine, so I had to stick with the scuffed loafers, but he had a pair of cotton socks that felt better than the polyester ones. I cleaned up pretty good.

"After dinner, I'm taking you to Grace Cathedral so you can get your 30-day chip."

Grace Cathedral sits on top of Nob Hill like a brick crown. In the basement, there's a multi-purpose room the size of a football field. Imagine a room that size filled with a thousand folding chairs, each seat taken by a reformed drunkard. That's the Grace Cathedral AA meeting. The speaker was an old shipyard worker who lost his job when they all moved to Alameda and Oakland. He lost his family when he drank instead of looking for new work. One of his kids found him lying in a gutter near Pier 37 and called the Rabbi. The Rabbi dragged him to an AA meeting, and his life changed. He slipped a few times, but he knew the right thing to do was to stay sober with help from his God. It was a good story.

After that, they asked everyone who had 30 days of sobriety to come up front and take a chip. It was a plastic poker chip that said "AA Grace Cathedral" on the front and "30 Days" on the back. I felt proud when I took it. I looked out into the audience, seeing a thousand people applauding for me and the 20 other people who took a chip, and it felt strange. Like a room of a thousand people were prouder of me than my parents had ever been. It was like I needed those people to stay proud of me. I needed to stay sober.

After the meeting, Greg and two of his friends took me out to coffee at an all-night diner on Mason and Eddy. We had to walk down Nob Hill until we started passing the cardboard boxes where drunks slept. Seeing those bums was a reminder of where I was headed before Greg had picked me up off the baseball diamond and dragged me to the hospital.

Stirring sugar into my coffee, I said, "I was lucky Greg found me."

An older queen named Norman chuckled nervously. "You decide if it's lucky after a few days in that house with him."

Greg swatted Norman playfully. "Knock it off!"

The other guy, Hector, was my age. He was Norman's boyfriend, I found out. Hector was Salvadoran. He had lived with his family in the Mission and helped out at their restaurant. He said they threw him out when he told them he liked guys. He drank, became a drunk, and lived on the street. One night, in a stupor, he found an AA meeting when he was looking for a toilet to throw up in. He looked pretty good that night under the fluorescent lights of the coffee shop.

"I've been sober for six months," he said, "And I love it."

Norman shrugged. "He's still on a pink cloud."

Hector blushed. "I can't help it. I never felt better. And then I found you." He leaned in for a kiss with Norman like it was normal. I guess in San Francisco, it is. I felt uncomfortable and jealous at the same time. I saw what Hector and Norman had, and it looked pretty good.

I looked out the window and saw the lights of a liquor store with a flashing Coors sign. It beckoned me like a devil on my shoulder. I focused my attention back on the coffee. I shifted in my seat, which must have somehow tightened the leg of my pants. Hector did a double take.

"Is that you?" His eyes were fixed on my thigh.

I nodded.

"Can I touch it?"

I frowned. "What, right here in the restaurant?"

Hector nodded vigorously.

I looked at Norman. "Isn't that cheating?"

Norman and Hector both laughed. Norman said, "We have an open relationship."

I hadn't heard that before, but I immediately knew what it meant. They fucked around on each other, and it was cool. "Holy shit, the gays have it good!"

More laughter. Hector said, "So, can I touch it?"

"Knock yourself out."

Hector placed his palm along the edge of my dick and curled his fingers. It felt good. I looked around. Nobody in the joint noticed, but Norman and Greg leaned over to see what was going on.

Norman whistled. "Holy shit, Pete. You've got an Anaconda down there!"

Greg said, "Can you say that louder, Norman? Someone in Boise, Idaho, didn't quite catch that."

I picked up Hector's hand and placed it on the table. "That's enough. I'm not walking out of here with a boner."

Greg said, "I think you'd fall over. That thing looks so damn heavy already."

I felt a rush of anger. I waited for it to subside. Then I said, "I know it seems like a good thing, but I don't always like it when people make fun of my size." The air grew tense.

Greg said, "Eleventh step. I'm sorry, that was mean of me. I hope I didn't hurt your feelings, and you'll find it in your heart to forgive me."

I remembered the 11th step was something about promptly admitting when you're wrong. I liked that. It felt like the way decent human beings acted toward each other.

"I accept your apology, Greg."

The tension in the air died down.

Hector said, "Do you like it when people admire it, though?"

I nodded. "Other guys I know just tease me about

it. I guess I kind of like it when guys are into it, you know, say nice things instead of teasing me."

Hector said, "It's the biggest one I've ever seen, and I haven't even seen it yet. Like that, right?"

I smiled. "Yeah, that's good. But not here in the restaurant."

"Why not?"

"I don't want to get a boner. Remember?"

Norman said, "Why don't you come back to ours?"

Greg bristled. "You know that's a bad idea."

Norman looked at me. "It's your body. What do you want to do with it?"

"I wanna fuck around since I can't get drunk. It's the next best thing."

Hector smiled. "This is going to be so much fun!"

Tenderloin Palace

❧

G reg made sure I had my set of keys and went back to his place. I could see he was frustrated. I think I would be, too.

Norman lived in the Tenderloin, a few blocks from the diner. It was one of those old apartment buildings from the 1920s. Tall, with a rickety old elevator. It was nicer than a lot of the places around it. Norman and Hector were on the top floor. Norman took my jacket while Hector excused himself to the shower. I was in a huge apartment with a view of the whole city in every direction. Out one window you could see North over the top of Nob Hill to Alcatraz. In another, you could see east to Telegraph Hill and Oakland beyond that. You saw the ocean out west and the Peninsula to the south. I grew up in the city, and I'd never seen all four directions in one place. I wandered from one end of the penthouse to the other, blown away.

I wondered how Norman could have such a nice place, so I asked him.

"I'm in entertainment," he said, "adult entertainment.

"You mean porno?"

He nodded. "Yeah. It's a booming business."

Hector came out of the shower naked. His body was thin and hairless. I liked everything about him except his dick, which was probably bigger than average. I didn't like looking at guys' dicks.

"Turn around, I said."

Hector's backside was soft and round. Like a girl's ass. I felt my cock leap in response. Hector saw and smiled.

"You like this?" He rubbed his ass.

" Uh-huh." I did. "Too bad."

Hector frowned. "What do you mean 'too bad'?"

I said, "I mean, I wish I could fuck you."

Norman put a hand on his crotch and squeezed. It was a fat bulge. "He's had a lot of practice. You'd be surprised."

In the bedroom, there was a leather hanging chair. Hector climbed up into it and put his feet through some stirrups. His asshole was on display.

"How is this gonna work?"

Norman said, "I like to watch. Don't worry, you won't even know I'm here. I might take a couple of photos if it's okay."

I shrugged. "Don't send them to the newspaper; I'll be cool."

After I said that, I felt kind of weird. *Was it a good idea to let him photograph me?* "Wait, what are you gonna do with them?"

Norman said, "They're for my private collection. They're Polaroids, one of a kind."

I shrugged again. "No prob."

Hector was impatient. "Come on, let me see it!"

I dropped my baggy pants, revealing my half-hard monster. Hector gulped. "Ay, papi. It's so...," he thought about it before he said, "Huge. And beautiful."

I got off on that, like I said. My dick started to grow and lift. Hector's eyes got wider as it got bigger and bigger. Norman left the room and came back with a can of Crisco.

"You're gonna need this." He handed it to Hector.

I could see Norman was fully hard in his pants.

Hector had a boner, too. I was ready to put it away, fig-
uring Hector would chicken out, but he said, "Come
here."

I came up close to him. He put a glob of Crisco on
my dick and massaged it. His hand felt small against my
cock. It took him about two minutes to grease me up.
By then, I was fully erect.

"Go slow."

I can't tell you how many times I heard a woman say
that. It was frustrating. I wanted to be able to shove it
in, but I couldn't. It was always a long, slow process.
And absolutely none of them ever let me go anywhere
near their ass. Hector was gonna be my first asshole if
he stayed the course.

He pulled the end of my dick until it rested against
his hole.

"Okay, go."

I leaned against his hole, surprised at how soft and
tight it felt against the tip of my dick. He nodded, so I
kept going. I felt the head get sucked inside him. His
asshole was a muscle, and it gripped me tightly. Pussies
couldn't do that. It felt fucking incredible.

My dick head is smaller than the shaft. As I pushed
a little deeper, Hector made a face. "Wait! Back up a
little!"

I pulled a couple of inches out until my head was
just inside him again.

Hector nodded. I pushed forward a little further,
then pulled back when I saw his face contort.

"No, keep going. Don't stop."

I pushed steadily until I hit a wall. Hector shook. I
saw a flash and heard a Polaroid snap to my left.

"Fucking beautiful," Norman said.

I was sort of bummed that Hector's asshole wasn't
even as deep as a pussy. The rest of my dick was out in
the cold. I pumped back and forth, finding my rhythm.

Then Hector said, "Okay, I'm ready."

I didn't know what he meant. I found out pretty

quick. He reached forward and held my thighs, pulling me towards him. With a loud 'Pop!' I pushed past something tight inside. Hector thrashed from side to side. I was about to pull out when he said, "Fuck! Fuck! No! Don't pull back. No! Stay there, please."

I was probably nine deep now, deeper than I'd ever been inside a woman. He pulled again, and I felt something I'd never felt before. My hips touched his skin. Then, I went deeper. I saw the head of my cock form an outline on his belly. It was so hot I felt my balls start to churn. Hector's dick went limp. I was sort of relieved. I didn't like looking at it. This way, it was kind of hidden between his thigh and groin. I pulled back a few inches and pushed in, fascinated by the bump in Hector's belly.

You don't miss what you never knew. I'd never been inside someone all the way. God, I didn't know how good it would feel. Hector's asshole twitched, grabbing the base of my cock in a rhythmic pulse.

I heard myself says, "Oh, shit. That's too fucking good."

Hector's eyes were glazed over like he was in a trance. I looked into his eyes while I humped him. Every so often, the light would come back in, and we connected. Then he'd go into a trance again.

Then Hector said something I'd never heard before. "Harder."

"Are you sure?"

"Fuck yes, dude. Harder!"

I took longer, faster strokes. Each time I popped in or out of that deep hole, I heard a snapping sound. Hector's belly muscles spasmed. I felt his insides churning and coiling around my cock. It was all too much.

"Hey. I think I'm gonna come."

Hector grabbed his dick and jacked it. I put my hand over it and pushed it away. "Wait til I'm done."

Hector nodded. I saw his dick was drooling pre-come. It was gross. I focused on his eyes. He was back in the room again, breathing hard, staring back at me. Flash, snap, whir! Another Polaroid.

I picked up the pace, taking very long strokes. Flash, snap, whir! Another one. Hector was crying softly, his lips moving like a silent Hail Mary. I leaned over and tried to kiss him, but he pushed my face away!

I pushed in all the way, ready to pop. Then I did; I was never turned on like this with a woman. I must have shot a gallon of come up there. It just kept coming and coming. Hector took his feet out of the stirrups and crossed his ankles behind my butt, pulling me as deep as I could go. Finally, the blasts subsided. I heard Norman make a cry and out of the corner of my eye, I saw a load sail skyward, landing on the carpet. I looked away, but Hector was playing with his big dick now. I looked up at the ceiling.

After a minute buried inside Hector, I felt hot come splash on my belly. Hector could see I didn't like it much, and he wiped it off with his hand. I looked away before he licked his fingers. I was down with this gay shit, but the big dicks and all the come was weird. I made a lady squirt once, but it was just a dribble compared to this shit. Still, it was worth it just to be able to get my whole cock inside.

Hector said, "You must have fucked a lot of ass. You're good."

I pulled out, letting my soft cock slap my thigh. "You're my first."

"Really?" He turned to Norman. "Honey, he's a natural."

Norman nodded. "I saw. He fucks like poetry."

Now, it was my turn to take a shower. My dick was greasy with Crisco, and it took a lot of soap to get it clean. When I came out of the shower, my clothes (well, Greg's clothes, really) were folded on a chair just outside the door. I put them on. Hector was out on the balcony smoking a cigarette. Norman was watching the late-night news. He looked up.

"Oh, you're out. Here, let me give you my card." He gave me a business card that read, "Norman Curry, The Tea Room," with an address on Eddy and a phone number.

"What's this for?" I asked.

He said, "If you need some extra cash, I got plenty of work for you. It pays well."

My job with the city paid pretty good, but it still would be cool to make some extra dough. "What kind of work?"

"Dancing, mostly. Maybe a little acting if you're up for it."

I stuffed the card in my pocket and said, "I'll think about it. I should probably get back to Greg's place."

Greg was asleep when I got back. The spare room was outside down a rickety, narrow flight of stairs. It didn't have heat but there were plenty of blankets. I fell into a dreamless sleep.

Popper Top

❧

In the morning, I followed the scent of bacon up the stairs to Greg's kitchen. He'd made a full breakfast for both of us.

"I have to go open the bookstore for my employee, but I'll be back in a bit."

I realized then that he owned the bookstore. "What's the name of your store?"

"It's called the Ben-Her. It's on Polk."

Polk Street was the other gay neighborhood. The Castro was kind of posh, and Polk Street was seedier.

I took Greg's plate and started doing dishes. Greg came in, put a hand on my shoulder, and said, "I like that I didn't have to ask. Thank you. I'll be back in a couple of hours. Make yourself at home; watch TV. There's soda in the fridge."

In the past 30 days, I hadn't been alone for more than a few minutes outside my locked apartment. Now that I was finally alone with my thoughts, they immediately turned to liquor. *We're at the top of Russian Hill. The liquor store's just a few blocks down a really steep set of stairs. I could go, drink, and be back before Greg got home. Would he smell it on my breath? Did I have any money? No.* All I had was a 30-day chip. That was God talking to me right there.

I felt guilty. When he got back, I told Greg about what happened.

"That's natural. You were tempted. You didn't yield. That's a good habit to build. Get tempted, let it pass."

I saw what he meant. In the hospital, there was no way I could get anything except maybe a sleeping pill or a Valium. Out here, booze was everywhere I turned. Up here on the hill, I was just far enough away to keep sober. I wasn't sure what I'd do when I went back to work.

Greg drove me to City Hall, where I got a certified copy of my birth certificate. Then, he drove me up to the DMV, where I applied for a new license. It was going to come in the mail in several weeks, but they gave me a temporary license on a piece of carbon paper.

Then we went to my bank out in the Richmond where they knew me, sort of. I explained what happened, and after signing a bunch of papers and leaving a thumb print, they gave me fifty dollars, some temporary checks, and a new passbook.

Next, Greg took me to the Castro to a men's shop. He insisted on paying for some new clothes for me. The shop guy was a fag — was gay. A real queen. He spent way too much time measuring my inseam. Twice, just to be sure. *Yeah, right.*

But the pants were nice. The shoes were great, too. He must have spent two hundred dollars on me. I felt really guilty, but I needed the help.

Then I asked him to take me to the Surplus Store on Market. There, I bought jeans, two pairs of coveralls, t-shirts, some Pendletons, and some waffle stompers. Work clothes.

I couldn't believe we got so much done in one day. Greg stopped on Polk to dip into the Ben Her and give the cashier his dinner break. Inside, there were a lot of strange guys wandering in and out of a room in the back.

"What's back there?"

Greg said, "Arcade. Film booths."

"Dirty films?"

"Yeah. Go on back. Check it out."

I went back there, and it was a goddamned orgy. Guys jacking off, fucking, and sucking everywhere. There were all these little booths showing movies, but nobody was watching them. I ran out of there. Greg smiled.

"See anything you liked?"

I said, "Too many dicks. Not enough ass."

Then my eyes landed on a box of those weird glass vials surrounded by green netting. The shit I had to pick up all the time at Collingwood.

"I see those all the time. What are they?"

Greg said, "We call them poppers. They're supposed to be for chest pain, but we use them for something else."

"They're a bitch to clean up. I'm afraid to ask what they're for."

Greg smiled mysteriously. "Given your preference, I don't think you need to know."

That irked me. "Well, now I'm confused so you better explain."

Greg said, "You're a total top."

I frowned. I had no idea what that meant, either.

"Sorry," he continued, "Uh, you're a top. It means you only fuck. You don't like to take it up the ass. They're for guys who do."

"Go on."

"Uh, well, bottoms, as we're called, need to relax during, you know. Poppers help with that."

"Can I try one?"

Greg sighed. "Some folks in AA would say you can't. I still need them sometimes. I like 'em big."

"So, can I try it?"

Greg looked around. The front was empty.

Here. I don't think you'll like it, though. Just crush

it between your fingers and inhale a couple of times. Here's a trash can."

I popped the glass and held it to my nose. It smelled like gasoline and burnt plastic. I took two deep breaths and tossed it in the garbage can.

"Nothing happened— whoa!" I felt my head throb like it was going to explode. It didn't hurt, but it felt really, really weird. Like I was drunk, it only lasted about 30 seconds.

Greg said, "Well, did you like it?"

I shook my head.

"Tops never do."

The whole front of the bookstore smelled like a chemical spill. That shit was pretty powerful. I leaned over the trash can and took another whiff, and my head throbbed again.

"Ugh!"

Greg laughed. "Don't worry, I don't think you're going to need them."

"'Cause I'm a total top."

"You catch on quick."

Our eyes met. We had one of those moments, the kind where it felt like we could kiss. But a customer walked in and bought a bunch of quarters for the booths in back. He gave me a long look. He was an older guy with gray hair and a trench coat. I looked away. I didn't mind him looking, but I didn't want to see that hungry expression on his face. Greg didn't have that. He had a friendly smile and a brightness in his eyes that comes with sobriety.

When the cashier got back, Greg took me to The Grubstake, an old railroad car they turned into a diner. We had burgers and fries and washed it down with Pepsi. The fries were the best I'd ever had. I wondered how I could have lived in San Francisco my whole life and never known about this place. I guess it was because I didn't want anyone thinking I was a fruitcake out on Polk Street.

After burgers, Greg took me to a night meeting at the Lutheran Church. It was all gay guys. A hundred heads turned to look at me when I walked in. I made a beeline for the donuts and coffee. AA coffee tastes better than regular coffee. I don't know why.

Opposites Attract

❧

After the meeting, we drove back to Greg's place. His couch was the expensive kind that feels good to sit on. My old couch was a beat-up thrift store couch. It had broken springs and felt like sitting on a park bench. Greg's was like a soft cloud rushing up to meet my butt. We watched *All In the Family*. Greg stretched out his muscly arms behind my head. His meaty legs hung open. I did the same. Our knees touched. I looked at Greg's profile. I realized he was beautiful. If he dressed like a girl, he'd be prettier than any woman I'd ever been with. But I didn't want him to dress like a girl. No, I liked him in those white tennis shorts with tan legs. He stood up to go to the bathroom, and the curve of his ass pinched the shorts, showing off his ass crack.

"Is your ass hungry?"

"Huh?"

"I said, is your ass hungry? Cause it's eating your shorts."

Greg smiled. He wiggled as he walked to the bathroom. Damn! Now that I'd had some ass, I wanted more. *What are the chances Greg's as good at taking a dick as Hector? He's all muscled up. His ass is probably so tight you couldn't get a pencil in there.* I heard Greg splashing around in the bathroom. The shower came on for a minute, but when he came out of the bathroom, his hair was dry.

Greg took his time sitting down so I could look at his ass some more. I grabbed my cock and rubbed it against my thigh. There was electricity in the air. When Greg turned to ask me a question, I held his jaw and kissed him. He lowered himself until he was on his back, looking up into my eyes while we locked lips. His big arms held me close.

My dick was so hard I didn't know if I could get it out of my pants. I unbuttoned and unzipped, pulling them down my legs. My dick was still trapped at the knees. Greg helped me until they unbundled, and my dick popped out.

"Holy shit!" Greg's eyes took it all in. "It's gigantic. And so fucking pretty."

I throbbed hearing that. Something about a guy seeing my cock and admiring it turned me on. I moved my hips until my cock was on his chin. He craned his neck and put the head in his mouth. I loved how he looked with his lips stretched tight around my cock. He shifted so he could take more. He kept taking more and more. His throat was wide open. I could see my dick bobbing at his Adam's apple. Just like Denise, he took my cock in both hands and stroked me off. He pulled it out of his throat and took a few breaths before going back down.

He was wearing one of those cowboy shirts with pearl snaps. He used one hand to tear it open. I got my first glimpse of his bare chest. His tits were huge. Not like a woman's, but just as beautiful. I rotated so I could fuck him from above and lean down to suck on a nip-ple. I saw a wet spot in his tennis shorts. That was okay. I liked that I was getting him wet.

From that new angle, I was able to fuck his throat. He took it like a champ. He coughed up some spit a few times, but he didn't quit. I kept staring at that wet spot, trying to figure out why it looked so hot. Then I realized it. He had no bulge at all. I liked that.

”Take off your shorts.”

He undid them and pulled them down, showing his bright blue underwear. I couldn't wear underwear. There was nothing in my size. His underwear was the sexy kind like European guys wear. They were soaked with his juice. And they looked almost empty. It made me curious.

”Let me see.”

He shook his head.

”Come on, Greg. Drop your drawers.”

He took my dick out of his mouth and said, “There's nothing to see.”

”How do you know what I like?”

Greg was beet red, and it wasn't just from blowing me. If you looked up shame in the dictionary, it would just be a picture of his face.

”I — I have the opposite problem.”

My cock throbbed just hearing it. He saw that.

I said, “Maybe it ain't a problem at all.”

Reluctantly, he lifted his heavy ass off the couch and pulled down his underwear, revealing a little tiny penis about the size of a clitoris. I swooned.

”Oh, fuck, that's beautiful.”

He said, “You've got to be kidding.”

Greg looked at my face and saw that I was serious. I stared at that little cock and knew I wanted to taste it. I bent over and scooped it up between my lips, letting my tongue roll over the tiny head and mouse balls. Greg shuddered and moaned.

It didn't take a minute to make him come. I was surprised how much came out of something so small. It tasted like I thought snow might taste. It wasn't weird or gross. I kept licking and sucking until Greg pounded my back.

”Stop! It's too sensitive!”

I pulled back. "I'm sorry, dude. It's just so fucking beautiful. You're fucking beautiful."

Greg sat up. He got on all fours, showing me his ass. It was round and muscular, with a deep crack. Instinct caused me to lean in, bury my nose in the crack, and lick his hole. It was clean and smelled like Dial soap. It tasted like a penny. The hole was tight, but it gave way to my tongue. I licked and spat, loosening that hole. I wanted in there so bad.

"Come on, let's go to my bed." He led me by the hand, his ass muscles tightening and loosening with each step until he hopped up on the bed, face up, legs in the air. As I continued to eat his ass, he lowered his legs to rest on my shoulders. I stood up, and he was in position.

"Open that drawer." He pointed to the bedside table. Inside was a tube of K-Y Jelly. My old friend. It had helped me get halfway inside the handful of women who hadn't run away screaming. I put a blob on Greg's asshole and pushed it inside with two fingers. He was a big guy, and my fingers fit just fine. I put in a third. He couldn't push back against the slippery K-Y, so I put in a fourth. I felt a little resistance. I spread my fingers apart like I'd done with my girlfriends. He didn't put up any sort of fight. He smiled at me and nodded. He was ready.

I slicked up my cock with lube and put the head at his hole. As I expected, the head went in pretty easy. Greg winced, but it was just a second and he was smiling and nodding.

"There's poppers in that drawer."

I handed him one, and he snapped it. I got a whiff, and it made my boner harder.

"Okay, go."

I pressed forward. Greg tapped my thigh, and I stopped.

"Stay right there. Oh god, yes, right there." I was

maybe two inches in, maybe three. Was that as far as he'd let me go? Nope. He took another whiff.

"Okay, keep pushing. I'm good now."

Oh, man, it felt good sliding into him. I hit the back and tried to turn the corner, but he held my thigh. Greg was over six feet tall, not like short Hector. His ass was probably an inch deeper. But there was another hole in there, and I wanted in.

"Can I keep going?"

Greg inhaled another gulp of poppers and lifted his side so I could go deeper. I found that second hole and pushed. Greg sucked his teeth and screwed up his face. But he didn't put a hand on my thigh. So I kept going. Pop! I was in. I slid forward quickly, causing Greg to gasp and thrash.

"Oh shit, man, am I hurting you?"

"Yes! But it hurts so damn good. Oh fuck, that's it. Right there. Oh god, right there, right there, right there." I guess I'd found the spot. I started to fuck. I made sure to hit that same spot deep inside him as I dragged my cock back and forth. His guts twitched and twisted, massaging my cock with his insides. *Fuck all those bitches who wouldn't let me fuck 'em in the ass.* This was the best feeling in the world. And it felt even better because Greg was moaning and asking for more!

Greg's guts were churning, but so was his butthole. The damn thing kept squeezing and squeezing like he couldn't help it. It was amazing. When our eyes connected, Greg was there looking at me a hundred percent. He didn't go somewhere else. He was in the room with me, smiling. We were each getting satisfaction from the other. It was a miracle of nature. *How did I not realize I was queer? There, I said it. I'm queer.*

Greg pulled his legs back until his knees were by his ears. It gave me a great angle to fuck him hard and fast. So I did. He thrashed from side to side, screaming out, "Yes! Yes! Deeper"

It was music to my ears. Not like all the times I only

ever heard, "No! No! Stop!" I fucked him silly. His body convulsed in spasms of pleasure. Then I felt it. That tingling in my balls as they drew up closer to my body.

I said, "I'm close."

"So am I."

He'd come once already, and he still hadn't touched himself; there was no way he could be close. I looked down, and his tiny pecker was hard and throbbing. I put my hand on it, but he pulled it away. "It'll happen on its own."

He still had that crushed popper in his hand. I think most of it had spilled out on the bed, but he held it under his nose one last time, smiling and closing his eyes. Then I felt it; his hole relaxed. It was like when you let go of an untied balloon. I felt all the come rush up my shaft at once and empty into his guts. At the same time, I felt hot spurts on my belly and chest. He was firing off a second load with no hands. It made me come more and harder. Greg's hard, muscular belly heaved and fell in rhythm to my jizm. I licked his right nipple, then gently bit it. He rubbed my head, running his fingers through my hair.

"Stay inside me."

I shifted positions so we could spoon. I fell asleep with my dick deep in his ass. When I woke up hard the next morning, it was still in there, ready for another round, so we fucked again. Afterwards, I held Greg against me, full of energy, ready to go again. We did it again.

Greg made breakfast. While I ate the best omelet I'd ever tasted, he said, "You can stay with me as long as you like. And you don't have to stay in the spare room."

"What's the rent?"

Greg grinned. "When you're ready, we can split it. I pay $450.00. Do you think you can afford $225.00?"

"Hell, yes!"

Joe Gardner

Saturday night, that urge for booze came down hard. I told Greg.

"I've got an idea. It's a surprise."

We got in his car, and he drove to the Castro. He parked right at my job site at Collingwood Park.

"What the hell, Greg? Why would you drag me here?"

Greg smiled. "We're not going to the park."

The Collingwood Rec Center lights were on. A crowd of gay guys was streaming in. I'd seen it one night when I lost my hat on Friday and went back on Saturday. I never knew what they were doing. But I smelled coffee, and I knew it was an AA meeting.

Inside was a madhouse. Queens were shrieking and telling stories. There were maybe two hundred guys, all of them gay. I felt another rush of emotion. I fought back tears. All this time, the answer had been about ten feet away from work. I had to go back to work on Monday. I thought it was the last place I wanted to be, but it was just where I belonged.

The speaker was telling my story. He thought he was straight for years and drank to get rid of that weird feeling that something wasn't right. He came out of a drunk blackout in a locked hospital and met a guy there who turned him on to gay sex. He was only in it for the sex at first, but then he realized it was love that was missing. He'd never been able to love a woman, but he found the right man, and they were still together after twenty years. I was blown away.

I turned to Greg and said, "Will you stay with me for twenty years?"

He patted my hand. "One day at a time, buster."

I started working again that Monday. I hadn't done the job sober, and it was a lot easier. I didn't mind picking up after the guys who fucked there at night. I get it. Sex with men is great. Why not do it wherever and whenever you can?

I didn't miss the work in Golden Gate Park with my old buddies. Most of them weren't my friends; they were just guys I drank with, except maybe Howard Bairfield. He was a cool black dude who tried to talk me into quitting drinking a bunch of times.

Still, I was making real friends in AA. It was hard to understand a lot of the God stuff because I'd given up on God about the same time I gave up on Santa Claus. But the rest of it made sense, and most of the guys there were trying to be better people. That meant a lot to me.

Driving a tractor mower while sober became dull and monotonous. I wanted something to keep my mind busy now that I wasn't drinking. The hard work was good for my body, at least. Without the hundreds of extra empty calories in beer and whisky, I toned up, lost a bunch of belly fat, and started to look really good. The guys in gay AA were slobbering over me. They wanted to drag me away from Greg and have their way with me. I found it weird at first, but after a few weeks of touch-feely talking with the men, I was learning to love the attention. It kind of put me on a natural high. Hands around my biceps, a playful pat on the rump, a hug that lasted longer than it should – these guys were desperate to fuck. But from what I could tell, not many of them had a beautiful little piece of meat like Greg's.

The last thing I wanted was a big dick slapping my face or trying to fuck me in the butt. No, Greg was the perfect lover. His ass was smooth and round; that hole puckered back up after every fuck.

The gardening was a good gig money-wise, but like I said, I was getting bored. I talked to Greg, and he agreed it was okay to give Norman a call about that side job he'd mentioned. Greg felt the need to warn me.

He said, "Norman's a bit of a trickster. He's not gonna feed you booze or drugs, but he might exploit you sexually."

"But I like the attention. And I doubt any of the guys are gonna have that perfect little dick like yours."

Greg nodded. "No, I'm probably the most cursed fairy in town."

I punched his shoulder playfully. "Curse? It's a god-damned blessing! I love the whole half-inch."

Greg blushed. "I don't think I've ever met a guy who felt that way until you."

"Trust me, it's perfect, bro. I never woulda stayed gay if I hadn't met a guy hung as small as you."

I think it was like a revelation for Greg. Having the complete opposite problem, I had never really put myself in his shoes. I loved to fuck pussy; then I found ass. *Did Greg wish he could fuck an ass, too? It would be impossible.*

I asked, "Dude, do you wish you could fuck me?"

Greg shrugged. "I gave up on that so many years ago, I can't count. It's hard being gay and hung so small. We queers are super-obsessed with our bodies. I hear them whispering about me."

I said, "Dude, they whisper about me, too."

He said, "It's different. You're the ideal. You're everything they want. You can't be too big."

"Trust me, you can."

Greg smiled. "Yeah, if anyone was, it'd be you."

That hurt a little, but probably not as much as it would hurt if I said he was too small. I got it. Manliness and dick size were proportional in the gay world. It was different with women. I felt really bad that Greg had to live with that his whole life. Thank God he found me!

On Wednesday, the forecast was a blazer. On days like that, I braved the morning fog in nothing more than my coveralls and the only pair of underwear that could hold me, a pair of BVDs that I got in the seconds pile at Penney's. The crotch had been sewn wrong. It was a gift from one of my girlfriends. I had to dress light. I wouldn't risk passing out again.

On my break, I worked up the courage to give Norman a call. He said I could come in that very day.

"What time do you finish up at Collingwood Park?"

I said, "I start pretty early now, so like 3:00 pm."

Norman said, "Perfect! Be at the Tea Room on Eddy between Mason and Taylor at 4:00 pm. We have an early bird special on Wednesdays, so it should be ideal."

That was near the Powell Street cable car turnaround. An hour would be plenty of time.

The problem was a few days before, a sprinkler broke at work. As luck would have it, at 2:45 I was packing it in to leave when the sprinkler repair guy showed up.

"Dude, what the fuck? I'm off in 10 minutes!" I was freaking out about being on time.

The sprinkler guy gave me the once-over. "What the fuck do you care? You're gonna get some sweet time-and-a-half."

I didn't dare tell him I was moonlighting. That could get me fired. I called Norman to tell him the situation, but nobody picked up. *Fuck!*

Then the sprinkler guy says he needs my help digging it out. My tractor-mower must have run over it the wrong way and cracked the pipe underneath. But we only had one shovel.

I said, "I'll dig, you scoop it out."

"No way. You do it. You broke it."

I cursed under my breath, but it had to be done. I

got on my knees in the mud and scooped out the dirt he loosened with his shovel until the broken pipe was exposed. It was 3:45 when he was done cutting and soldering the new pipe. I didn't even thank him. I ran to the tool shed and washed my hands. I couldn't get the mud out from under my fingernails; I was pouring down sweat, and my coveralls were caked with mud. And god damn, I wasn't wearing street clothes underneath.

The trolley took ages to get there, and it went extra slow around the subway construction site at Van Ness. It must have been almost 5:00 pm when I finally got to the turnaround. Between my filthy clothes and my extreme tardiness on day one, I knew it was hopeless. Still, I ran as fast as I could the few blocks. More sweat. Mud trickling in my eyes. I was a goddamn mess.

I stepped inside the Tea Room. I'd never seen anything like it. There was a gay fuck film on a big screen. Every seat in the theater was taken, and guys were standing in the aisles. Almost everyone was jacking off or rubbing their crotches. I looked for the office, but Norman had already spotted me and come down. He looked me over.

I said, "Norman, I'm so sorry, man. There was an emergency at work."

Norman shrugged. "Is that what you're wearing?"

I groaned inside. "Yeah, sorry, man, I only got my BVDs under here, and they barely even hold my junk. It might fall out."

I waited for him to fire me. Instead, he said, "Perfect. Perfect. From now on, when you're here, you're dressing like this. But add a T-shirt because you want more time. And I got the perfect stage name. Joe Gardner. Cool?"

I was stunned. "You mean, I gotta be all dirty like this?" I didn't understand the t-shirt comment, either, but I had too many questions.

Norman said, "Are you kidding? These guys will eat

it up! Look at you. You're so fucking hot. You smell so good I got a boner now. Oh man, you're gonna be a hit."

I wasn't sure where I was supposed to work. I'd been to the Lusty Lady, where you paid a dollar a minute to see a girl behind glass. I figured that was the job. But then the film ran out, and stage lights came on. Some crappy disco came on.

An emcee boomed over the loudspeaker. "Ladies and Gentleman, it's time for the Gaiety Follies! Please welcome to the stage Harry Cox!"

A big, hairy dude got up and started dancing to the beat. He was in boots, a T-shirt, and jeans. He swayed his hips, showing off his boner bulge. An old man came forward with a dollar bill and tucked it into the guy's waistband, petting his crotch. The dancer smiled and slowly lifted his t-shirt, revealing his hairy belly. This was like a queer version of the striptease at the Naked I on Broadway.

I said, "Norman, I don't really know how to dance."

Norman said, "I don't think anyone's gonna notice when you get those loose coveralls off."

The hairy guy twirled his t-shirt on one fat finger and tossed it offstage. Guys were coming forward with bills and rubbing his tummy. It was wild. I like smooth guys with little dicks, obviously, but Harry Cox was pretty sexy all the same. I liked the way he moved. Slowly, he opened his fly, starting with the top button. *More guys, more dollars. Now I get it.* That t-shirt had earned him a few extra bills.

One by one, the buttons came down as greedy hands stuffed bills into the waistband of his underwear. Then, when the fly was open all the way, he yanked the front of his jeans. In one motion, the jeans just came off. They must have had snaps on the legs or something. His legs were hairier than the top half of his body. I guess some guys are into that because they came rushing forward, taking liberties with his underwear by stuffing bills in the leg openings instead of the waistband. He didn't mind. He just kept encouraging the audience and more bills filled his underpants. He pulled them out and stuffed them in his boots. Then he let his underwear drop to his ankles. His dick was semi-hard, maybe six-and-a-half inches. The audience cheered. He stepped out of the underwear, hooking it on one boot and kicking it offstage. He turned around and bent over, spreading his hairy cheeks to reveal a furry hole. From that angle, where I couldn't see his dick, I got a little turned on. *Hell, I'd fuck that hole if he'd have me.*

He turned back around, and now his dick was fully hard. He swayed his hips, jacking his dick. Guys stepped forward. I thought they were just getting a closer look until he shuddered and sprayed a big wad of cum all over the front row and the standees. Cheers, then the spotlight came down. It was pitch black. Then, a movie came back on, bathing the audience in flickering reflections from the silver screen.

Norman turned to me. "So, kid, what do you think? You got the nerve?"

I wasn't sure I did, but I knew I liked attention, especially from a room full of gay guys. That outweighed any stage fright.

"Yeah, Norman. Piece of cake."

"You're up next."

Backstage, there was another guy. He was short, buffed, and hairless, like Hector. He had copper-colored hair with freckles. He smiled at me.

"You must be the new guy." He extended a hand. "I'm Dorian, but they call me Red Fox. Before you ask, yes. The carpet matches the drapes." I admired his freckled skin. He had a creamy white complexion underneath. His little body looked like a statue.

Red said, "I hear you're packing some serious heat. I'll believe it when I see it. See this?" He pinched his leg, and I noticed a long, hard dick on his upper thigh. "I'm the biggest one here. I'll bet you can't beat me. I'm a show-er and a grower."

I shrugged. "I like 'em small."

Red said, "Ooh. You're one of those. Bisexual?"

I said, "Yeah. Look, I'm kinda nervous. I can't dance. Especially to disco."

Red said, "Tell the Emcee. You got time. I'll bet you like Rock."

I did. I found the emcee and asked him to play some Zeppelin. He nodded and pulled out my favorite, Led Zeppelin IV. "I got you," he said, "I know just the song."

He did. When the 20-minute reel ran out, the spotlights hit the stage.

"We've got a new one for you. Give it up for Joe Gardner!"

I froze. Red pushed me, and I stumbled out on stage. Then "When the Levee Breaks" started to play. It was my favorite song. I knew how to dance to this one. I shook my hips in time to John Bonham's incredible drums. It was like I went on autopilot.

Nobody came forward. I realized my coveralls weren't revealing enough. I lowered the zipper halfway, letting my abs show. Then I spread the front, showing off my big pecs. A few timid men stood and tucked bills into the pockets of my gardening suit. One of them sniffed my belly and swooned.

"God damn, you smell good!"

I guess some guys like a stinky, sweaty guy. When he said that, a few more guys came forward, breathing in my aroma and tucking bills in my pockets. I realized I needed to unzip a little more and show them some underwear. I lowered the zipper a little more, revealing the waistband. More guys came forward. I shrugged off the top half of the suit, revealing my biceps and full chest. Now, they were coming in a steady stream, tucking bills in my waistband this time.

One guy pulled it forward and got a peek. "Oh, sweet Jesus! Fucking huge!"

More guys stood up. I was still nervous and soft. I

wanted to put on a good show. Norman gestured from the back to hurry up. Shit! Then I saw a cute guy in the front row, tugging on a little one-inch dick. It was perfect.

I focused on him, rubbing my crotch. I felt my cock growing heavier, sagging in the underwear, pulling the waistline down. I realized my coveralls were never gonna make it over my boots, and I didn't want to lose the dancing rhythm. I shook my hips, and they fell to my ankles.

That's when I heard shrieks. It was a rush of men of all shapes and sizes. Yep, most fags love a big dick. It's just the way it is. But I kept my eyes on the little guy in front. His muscles flexed as he tugged on his tiny meat, holding it between his thumb and forefinger. I grew harder, still not at full mast but getting closer. Greedy paws showered me with bills as they copped a feel. I saw one guy's eyes roll up in his head like he was about to faint.

Norman made a jerk-off gesture from the back of the room. The song was about to end. Shit! It ended. The emcee quickly tugged the needle up, making a scratching sound, and put on Black Dog. It was good jack-off music. When I pulled my dick out, it was pretty hard. The little guy in the audience was pumping furiously on his tiny prick. I pointed my dick at him, holding my cock with both hands and pumping up and down; I focused only on him. Horny guys with their pants around their ankles pawed at my cock.

A bouncer appeared out of nowhere and pulled them back. "You know the fucking rules, gents. Knock it off!"

Out of the corner of my eye, I saw Red Fox standing in the wings. His face was crestfallen. I had dethroned him. That turned me on even more. I winked at him. He smiled weakly, rubbing his crotch. Yep, even he couldn't help but be turned on by my superior dick.

Back to the guy with the mouse dick. I stared into

his eyes like he was the only guy in the room. He looked behind him. Nope, it was him I was jacking off for. I saw a grateful tear in the corner of his eye. It turned me on even more. As the beautiful off-tempo drum rhythm of the song pounded in my ears, I felt a rising tide. This was it. I was close. Then the little guy closed his eyes and shot a huge load skyward. *Oh fuck!* There was something magical about a little clit dick squirting so much juice. It pushed me over the edge.

I aimed my first squirt right at him. Then I turned and fired off like a garden hose. All the attention, the thrill of being on stage, the feeling of superiority over Red, and the room full of guys blowing their load with me was intoxicating. I felt a rush as I sprayed the room. The audience roared and broke into thunderous applause, cheers, and catcalls. As "Black Dog" ended, I dribbled out my last load. The lights went out. I pulled up my coveralls and strutted offstage, winking again at Red, who patted me on the rear. The film came up. I never felt so good.

Pete, I think you found your calling.

⚜

GREG WAS WAITING FOR ME AT HIS HOUSE. "WELL, what did you think?"

I grinned. "I fucking loved it!"

Greg nodded. He seemed a little sad. "What's wrong?"

Greg shrugged. "I really like you, Pete. I took an inventory and discovered that I don't want to share you with people. I'm being selfish, and I'm sorry."

I put a hand on his shoulder. "Hey, hey, don't say that. There's nothing to be sorry for. You're just jealous."

Greg said, "Yeah, but those kinds of feelings are dangerous for an alcoholic. I need to admit it, and hopefully, over time, God will remove it."

I said, "It kinda turns me on that you're jealous. Makes me want to fuck you into a sense of security."

Greg raised an eyebrow. "Is that a threat or a promise?"

I tugged on my hardening cock. "Both."

After sex, I counted my money. I hadn't realized there were fives, tens, and even a twenty among all the bills. I'd made a little over a hundred dollars for a couple of hours of work! That was enough for rent. More than a day's pay that I'd get working for the city. Two nights of that and my rent would be paid. Plus, I still had that job with the city. I felt something I hadn't felt in years: hope.

Shooting Star

❧❧

I never got tired of shaking my ding-a-ling for those guys. It was only a challenge if I couldn't find a guy in the audience with a tiny dick, which was rare. On those days, I'd picture Greg in my head. It worked. Those days grew even rarer after rumors spread that I liked the little ones. If Greg knew how many tiny guys wanted my dick, he'd be jealous as fuck. I didn't know if I should keep it a secret. Norman said we make amends, except when to do so would injure others. He said it would hurt Greg and wouldn't make things any better for either of us. So I kept it a secret.

About a month after I started dancing, Norman took me aside.

He said, "I got the financing for a movie. I'm hoping I can cast Joe Gardner in the leading role."

I was dumb enough to ask, "What's it about?"

Norman chuckled. "Sex. Lots of sex. And I got an angle, too. You're only gonna fuck bottoms with little dicks. I'm calling it 'Joe Gardner - Big Hose, Little Fields?' Whadda ya say?"

I thought about my old friends and what they would say about me. I thought about my new sober friends and what they would say. Most of all, I thought about Greg and what he would feel seeing me doing that stuff with other guys. Norman could tell I was on the fence.

He said, "Look, Pete, it's your body. You choose what you do with it. Don't worry about what a room full of sober drunks might think. Let me ask you this: does fucking ass make you happy?"

I nodded.

He said, "Then be proud of it. Don't let someone else's opinion keep you from your own bodily pleasure. It's yours."

I said, "I kinda got a good thing going with Greg. A movie like this could really fuck it up."

Norman said, "Let me talk to him. Pretend this conversation never happened. Trust me. I think I got a solution that makes everyone happy."

Two days later, when I got home from the Tea Room, Greg was sitting on the couch. He patted the cushion and said, "Come, sit."

I was worried that Norman might have somehow fucked things up, but Greg's smile was genuine.

"Norman approached me with an idea. I said I wouldn't make any decisions about it until we discussed it."

I said, "What idea is that?" I was genuinely puzzled as to what Norman might have said.

Greg said, "He's doing something innovative. A film. It's something that hasn't been done in porn yet...at least not as far as I know."

I shifted uncomfortably on the very comfy couch. "Go on."

Greg said, "Look, there's got to be a lot of guys like you that like guys like me. Guys who like little dicks. He offered me a role in his new movie. He said he was going to offer you a spot in it, too. Like we'd get paid to fuck on camera."

I was surprised by that last bit. Now I understood Norman's tactics. *Get Greg in the picture and I'd put out on camera for sure.*

Greg continued. "I mean, it's totally up to you. I won't do it unless you do."

I said, "Is it just me and you? Is that the whole film?"

Greg shook his head. "It would need a few more actors. Norman wants to showcase a lot of guys with small dicks. Apparently there are quite a few who go to the Tea Room."

I said, "Yeah, I've seen a few."

Greg said, "Norman told me how you really attract them because you show them so much attention."

Shit. I should have been upfront about it.

I said, "Yeah. I wasn't sure how to tell you. I hope you'll forgive me."

Greg said, "Forgive you? Come on, what's to forgive? You've got a job to do. If looking at little dicks gets you off, then by all means get off!"

I said, "You're not jealous?"

Greg laughed. "Do you want me to be?"

I smiled and shook my head.

Greg said, "Good. Then stop worrying about it. So, do you want to do the film?"

I said, "Fuck yeah!"

❧❦❧

THE FIRST SHOOT WAS ON SUNDAY. IT WAS AT A LOFT on the top floor above the Ben-Her bookstore. It was empty. Some thing about how Greg couldn't rent it to tenants because of zoning laws around dirty bookstores.

When I got on set, Norman took me aside. "This is your first shoot, buddy. A few things. We have to do stuff from a few different angles. If you ever feel like you're gonna come, give the camera guy plenty of warning. Other than that, just keep that huge fuckin' cock hard and have fun!"

The camera guy was a film student with a 16mm camera he'd borrowed from San Francisco State. He was a skinny, goofy guy with glasses and curly hair. He was just the way I'd imagined a porn cameraman would look. The sound guy had a long, pointy microphone on a pole. He was a husky dude with a hairy chest. His jeans were tight and showed off a big soft cock on one leg. He was an actor too, named Bear Chess. I wasn't going to be in every scene - he was the hired gun for two other scenes.

I'd read the script, which was really more of an outline. I was confused, because the opening scene was one of the guys hitting on me in Golden Gate Park. *Didn't we have to shoot that first?*

I said, "Norman, what about the park?"

He patted my shoulder. "Hollywood Magic. We shoot the outdoor scenes next Sunday."

I felt like an idiot. *Of course you can shoot out of order. It's not like a home movie where the whole reel is just inside the camera. They cut it up and move shit around all over the place. Duh.*

So the first guy was Earl, a slender Asian boy with a smile that looked like he was always up to no good. They set up the lights and filmed him walking onto camera and kneeling in front of me. He had to kneel extra low so my crotch wasn't blocked by his head. We practiced a few times. There was a lot of shifting around. I started to lose my boner, so I asked Greg to pull out his dick and play with it. That kept me hard while we shuffled and cheated until the shot was exactly what Norman wanted.

Norman said, "Okay, Earl, action!"

Earl walked to where they'd put a little tape on the floor, knelt down, and started unbuttoning my coveralls. He reached inside and hauled out my cock, gasping when he saw it. His little hand felt good on my cock. He leaned forward and put the tip in his mouth.

"And...cut!"

What? It was just getting good. I was surprised.

The camera guy said, "Side shot. Resetting". We did the exact same scene from the side, but this time Earl kept going, putting inch after inch of my cock into his little mouth and down his throat. I looked over to Greg, but he was busy making himself a cup of coffee. *Fuck it. This feels too damn good.* Earl blew me for a minute until they had to change reels.

All the starting and stopping could have been a turn-off, but it was like a challenge to keep my boner going. I'd slap it around a bit between takes. Earl and I ended up on the bed, and that's when the scene got really hot. Earl took off his slacks, revealing that he was wearing sheer women's underwear. I wasn't expecting that. My cock leaped off my lap as I looked at his tiny penis through the sheer fabric.

Norman shouted, "Great! Can you keep doing that?"

I could. I flexed my cock muscle, and my dong lifted again. Earl ripped his panties, letting his little cock flop out and exposing his perfect little ass. My cock probably grew an extra inch right then!

Earl took the lead. He stood facing me, his legs straddling my hips. He lowered himself until he could reach the head of my cock, then lifted it up, straightening his legs so he could get the tip in his hole. It was already slick with grease. As he sat down, I felt the hole grip the head of my dick, then the top of the shaft. Earl sobbed like a mother whose daughter had just drowned. Bear gave a thumbs up to Norman, who looked pleased.

Earl sat harder, taking another inch in his hole. Our eyes connected as he sat down little by little. All the way down, he gave off cries of pain. When I turned the corner, he shrieked. But he kept going. When he got to the bottom, I could see where the head of my cock was pushing his stomach out a little. It was so great, I couldn't help myself.

"Oh shit, that's hot."

Norman made a motion to continue talking.

I said, "You like that big fat cock in your tight little hole? You feel it in your guts?"

Earl nodded. "Yes, sir. Fuck me, sir."

I put my hands under his butt and lifted him an

inch or two, then dropped him. He squealed and snorted like a pig. His eyes glazed over as he entered the zone.

I pushed him forward until he was flat on his back, and then I rose to my knees. The cameraman swiveled to catch all the action as I started to fuck the little guy. My cock rubbed against the torn fabric of Earl's panties, so I ripped them more.

I was into it now. I kept fucking Earl, watching my dick press up against his belly from the inside. It reminded me of that scene in The Exorcist where Regan's stomach gets raised welts that say, "Help Me". Earl probably needed help, too. His eyes fluttered, showing only the whites, just like in the movie. He was possessed by my cock. He reached up one hand and pinched my nipple. I slapped it away. "Keep still, bitch."

I was getting into the role. I was more like the city gardener that Greg met the day I passed out. I was rough, angry, and raw.

Norman called out, "Cut!"

Had I done something wrong? Why did we stop?

"Reset, let's get the c-cam."

I stepped back from the bed while the camera guy got on the ground. When Norman called action, I stuck my dick into Earl again, slowly, letting the whole length go in. Then, I pulled back slowly before going back in. I picked up the pace until the entire length of my cock was sliding in and out of Earl's asshole.

The cameraman said, "Holy shit." I looked down at him and smiled. He waved my face away.

"Don't look in the camera."

I didn't need to. I was looking at Earl's little nib dribbling a long, sticky trail of clear precum, wetting what was left of his panties. That was what sent me over a precipice.

"I'm gonna come soon," I told Norman, just as promised.

Norman said, "Pull out but don't come. Hold it over Earl, so your balls are centered in the camera."

All the tech talk had made the moment go away anyway. We switched angles again, so the camera was over my shoulder. I fucked Earl some more for continuity. The camera guy whispered in my ear, "Is that your dick against his stomach?"

I nodded.

"I've never seen that. Let me zoom in."

After a minute, I pulled out my cock and jerked it. Earl diddled his dick, saying, "Yeah, man, come on me. Come on me."

I looked at his little dick and pretended we were at the Tea Room. I thought about my cock in his ass, in Greg's ass, in whatever ass was coming next. It took a minute or so, but I finally felt the spooge building up in my balls.

"Cut! We gotta change reels."

Again, the moment subsided. When the fresh roll of film was in the camera, I closed my eyes and pictured Greg spreading his ass cheeks for me, his little dick hanging between his huge meaty thighs. I imagined putting my hand over the tiny mound and rubbing it. My breath grew faster. I looked down at Earl playing with his dick. My breath came faster in shallow breaths. Bear pointed the microphone at me, capturing the sounds of my breathing.

"Oh, shit, I'm gonna come!"

Earl said, "Do it, come on me!"

Because I had been so close a few times already, when I finally came, it was an avalanche. I must have shot a quarter cup of the stuff all over Earl's face and chest. He licked it up like a pie in the face. We stayed like that an unnaturally long time before Norman called cut.

Norman pulled me aside. "You're going to be a superstar. I hope you're ready for it."

I wasn't sure I was, but I didn't care. I was getting paid a ton of money to fuck guys with little dicks.

I said, "Norman, I might have come too much. I'm not sure I can do it like that again."

Norman said, "We do spooge pickup shots Sunday after next. But I'll bet you can come another gusher today with Greg."

I thought about him. *His muscly ass always makes me come, doesn't it? Even after a big show at the Tea Room.* I was up for it.

Norman said, "I need you to fill in for Bear Chess as the sound guy now. You're doing boom for his scene with Greg."

His scene with Greg? I don't remember that in the outline! Fucking Norman. He was such a manipulative shit.

I thought watching that big dude fucking my man would piss me off, but it didn't. I knew Greg was pretending like it was enough. The guy's dick was huge but nothing like mine. Greg opened his legs and wrapped them around Bear. The sounds he made were not like what I heard when I fucked him. He was faking it. I think.

Seeing Bear's big dick sliding in and out of Greg's ass was mesmerizing. I started to get hard watching it. When Bear finally came all over him, I could feel my dick straining against my coveralls. I was ready to fuck again.

In my scene with Greg, things got heated. I could still feel Bear's come in Greg's hole. I got so turned on, I wouldn't stop when Norman yelled, "cut!" so they just had to improvise and move stuff around.

Greg's gaping hole tightened around my cock head each time I pushed in. When I pulled out, it gave out a groaning noise and stayed open for a few seconds. I'd never fucked Greg when he was all warmed up by another big dick. Even with the film crew in the room, I was harder than ever before. Being filmed turned me

on. When I came, it flew past Greg and hit the camera
lens. That was a wrap.

A Big Scene

❧

The following Sunday, all anybody talked about was my dick. I was like a zoo animal. We were in a part of Golden Gate Park I had always avoided. It was a series of trails between the Eucalyptus, away from the roads. I'd known it was a place where fags, uh, gay guys met up and fucked. We called it "Fairy Woods". It was weird to be back. I prayed the other guys I'd worked with weren't around.

We had a few scenes here, none of them with sound. In one scene, Earl watches me work. He makes eye contact and puts his hand on my crotch before we supposedly go back to his place to fuck. In another, Greg is taking a piss, and I catch him. Instead of reprimanding him, I take out my cock and start to jerk it. The scene is shot over Bear's shoulder. He's my coworker, and he wants in on the action.

We started that over-the-shoulder shot. No sooner had Bear pulled out his meat Howard Bairfield showed up with a leaf blower. Howard was the only one of my coworkers who only knew me as Big Peter the Drunk but cared about me. He was a big black dude with a natural. The stunned look on his face turned to anger.

"What the fuck is going on here, Pete?"

Dick in hand, I said, "We're making a movie."

Howard looked from one face to another. Bear

65

stuffed his cock back in his coveralls. Norman looked like he was gonna have a heart attack. You could hear the crunch of leaves as Howard shifted from one foot to the other.

Howard said, "A porno, huh? Where's the girls?"

I shrugged. "There aren't any girls in this one, Howard."

He said, "I oughta turn you in."

I saw a chain of events in my head ending with me going to jail, losing my city job, and having to do porn as my main hustle.

Then Howard said, "But how much you make for a thing like this?"

Norman said, "A few hundred dollars per scene. Are you interested?"

Howard had a wife and three kids. I knew he wasn't interested. I could almost hear the clang of the jail cell door when he said, "Getting paid to fuck some ass? Hell, yeah!"

I said, "But Howard, it's a queer film."

Howard put his hands on his hips and said, "Pete, you think I don't know that? I don't give a shit. I'd fuck a pretty little Chinese boy like him," he nodded towards Earl, "or whatever. Ass is ass. I still ought to report you, man. Don't you need a permit and shit?"

Norman said, "Here's my card. Give me a call. I'll make you a big star. Can we let this go unreported? I filed for the permit." *So much for rigorous honesty.*

Howard studied the card before putting it in his pocket. "Yeah, man, I don't give a shit. Just don't get me in trouble today. I never seen you. And I'll be calling you, for sure. Rhonda's pregnant with number four, and I ain't getting nothing."

I grinned sheepishly. "Number four, Howard? Congratulations."

Howard said, "Yeah. And hey, you look better, brother. You quit drinking?"

I nodded.

"Good for you, Pete! Rhonda always prayed for your ass on Sundays. She's probably doing it right now. I'll give her the good news." He picked up his leaf blower and walked over the hill and out of sight.

It was only a half-day shoot, but we got paid for a full day.

⚬⚬⚬

THE FOLLOWING SUNDAY, WE HAD A FEW PICKUP cumshots and what Norman called "The Big Scene." It wasn't on the outline he gave me. There were five actors: Earl, Bear, Howard, Greg, and me. In the first scene, I was standing over Earl, fake cum all over his body, when the door opens. In walks Howard. He's wearing a suit like he just came from church. He pushes me aside and fucks Earl. I'd never seen Howard's cock, but it was impressive. Not the kind I like, obviously, but big, fat, and good for porn. He was rock hard when he started fucking Earl. It didn't turn me on the way it had watching Greg get fucked. It did turn me on a little, though.

I watched them shoot a few angles, and then Norman said, "Greg, Bear, you're up."

The plot didn't make any sense. Greg and Bear just walk into the scene and join Earl and Howard on the bed. Howard pulls out of Earl and fucks Greg while Bear gives it to Earl. Now, seeing Howard fuck Greg, I felt my dick getting rock hard. Norman saw the tent in my coveralls and motioned for me to join in.

He said, "Pete, you're taking over for Howard, and Greg is gonna suck him. Bear, when you finish with Earl, you're going to do a DP."

I didn't know what a DP was. We stopped filming the two simultaneous sex scenes and just concentrated on Bear fucking Earl. Greg's arm had to be in the shot "for continuity," as the camera guy said, so he stayed on his back next to Earl.

Bear pulled out and shot his load. Earl's work was through, and Norman sent him home. Now it was time for 'the DP shot'.

Bear knelt over Greg's head and dangled his sloppy dick for Greg to clean it while Howard plowed his ass. My boner was back.

Norman said, "Get on your back. Howard, pull out. Greg, I want you to squat down on Joe's, uh, Pete's cock and take the whole thing, yeah?"

Greg sat on my cock, facing away from me, and let his body fall back onto my chest. I instinctively put my hands on his nipples and played with them, which caused him to wriggle a bit.

"Good," Norman said, "Bear, you go down his throat. You can do deep throat, yeah, Greg?"

Greg didn't answer, just proved he could.

"Alright, Howard, now you go in."

I was baffled, but Howard must have seen a lot more porn than I had. He knew what to do, and it blew my mind. While I was stretching Greg further than any normal man could take it, Howard came in with his big, black dick and started cramming it in there. I felt his big dick touch mine and started to lose my boner. But as the head forced its way into Greg, I felt a rush of lust. I'd never felt another man's cock against my own. To have it happen inside Greg's ass was a perfect introduction. Greg cried out in real pain, but it subsided. I felt Howard slide in deep along the length of my shaft until his balls hit mine. He had pushed a little way past that second hole.

Bear pulled his cock out of Greg's mouth and shot a load across his stomach. Norman sent him home, too, with an envelope full of cash.

Howard was a fuck machine. He pounded Greg with a rhythm, unlike anything I'd ever done. It was long, long, short-short-short, then it was long-short-long-long-long...like a jazz song. I mean, you couldn't tell what he was gonna do next. And he was pressed up against my dick, inside Greg, making me feel like I was part of the rhythm. I'd always liked Howard the best of the crew in Golden Gate Park, and now I was bonding with him in a strange new way.

Howard said, "Yeah, bitch, take it!" He pounded and pulled, tugged and pushed, all the while bringing me closer to coming with the friction of his fat dick pressed against mine.

Greg said, "Yes! Oh fuck, yes!" He ground his ass into my crotch, fingering his little piece of meat. I felt it run down the crease of his thigh onto my leg. It pushed me closer.

Howard shocked me when he put his tongue in my mouth. It was an unexpected connection with my past. He tasted different, smelled different, fucked different. It was a new experience, and instead of frightening me, it made me harder. I felt Greg's hole give way to my increased girth as he let out a sob of pleasure.

"Oh shit, I'm coming," Howard announced it before he could pull out. I felt the hot sperm coat my shaft. He cried out in loud grunts as he pushed his come into Greg, who writhed in ecstasy against my chest.

Norman said to me, "Stay inside. We'll get the after-shot." I hadn't heard the term before, but I suspected I knew what it meant. Howard grew soft, pulled out roughly, and stepped away from the camera. The feeling sent me over the edge. Apparently, it sent Greg over, too.

Greg said, "I'm coming! Shit, I'm coming!" He tightened his abs in a situp, and I felt his tiny clit of a dick spray past his head, landing on my forehead. More came in giant spurts. That did it; I was falling now. Falling into an orgasm.

The camera came close up on my balls as they pumped like a bee stinger, flooding Greg's insides.

Norman said, "Pull out and keep coming."

I did. A flood of jizz poured out of Greg's gaping hole and landed in my lap. My cock towered over us both, producing a fountain of sperm that soaked us both.

Norman said, "Lift his knees so we can see his ass."

I couldn't see it at the time, but in the editing room, I learned that his hole was as big as the eighteenth hole on the city golf course. The rest of my cum mingled with Howard's as it trickled and flowed out of Greg's gaping ass.

Sweaty and exhausted, Greg collapsed back onto my chest. We stayed there, breathing in heavy pants of joy. An electric pulse traveled back and forth between us as Greg shuddered and shook involuntarily, his hips twitching in such a way that his ass ground into my pubes.

When Greg's shudders subsided, then stopped, Norman yelled, "Cut!"

Epilogue

It's been nearly two years, and me and Greg are still together. We do porn together as a couple, "Joe and Jacob." We dropped the Gardner so I could play other roles.

Greg can't get enough of my dick. We fuck every day, on and off camera. Sometimes we fuck two or three times a day. He was made for me.

There's no hesitation now. He's loose enough that I can just stick it in and start fucking. That was a dream of mine, and it came true. He's used to me.

Each time we fuck, we get a little closer to one another. I haven't had a drink since the day we met. We call that our anniversary. It's kind of perfect because I got my one-year chip on our anniversary, and I'm about to get my two-year chip next month, God willing.

Working in porn, the sex is different. You don't have as much spontaneity, and there's all those starts and stops. It's good, and it pays well.

Off camera, the sex is great, but my favorite part is the cuddling afterwards. Sometimes I spoon him from behind, and sometimes he holds me in his big arms and I curl up between his muscular thighs, letting his tiny pecker rest against my butt. It's the kind of love I didn't know existed. When I was a drunk, I couldn't love myself or anyone else. Greg changed all that. I still call him a guardian angel when I talk about him to other people. He won't let me call him an angel.

"I'm a man, just like anyone else."

And I say, "Yeah, but you're my man."

The End

Edging the Lawn

CHUCK IDGAF

Hi, my name is Charlie. I graduated high school in the late 80s.

I have a summer birthday. Now, usually, that means you're one of the youngest in your class. However, my father was obsessed about me excelling in school, so he decided to hold me back and start a year late. His thought was that if I were the youngest one in class, I might have difficulty, especially when it came to maturity. I'll admit, it did pay off a couple of times.

I was one of the smaller kids when I was young, and a big sissy about bugs and dirt and stuff, and not good at sports. I could have been an easy target for the bullies. Fortunately, when puberty hit, I started the school year as one of the bigger kids after a large growth spurt over the summer. This meant that entering junior high, I wasn't going in with a target on my back.

Turning 16 was a great year, also, because I had my driver's license before everyone else at school.

My parents had to get me a car because I transferred to the fancy high school that offered all the advanced classes. My father, being cheap, got me an old, beat-up pickup truck. I think mostly because he wanted a pickup available to him for all of his odd jobs and side projects.

My father wouldn't let me get a part-time job during high school because he thought it would affect my grades.

The social impact of this meant I had very little cash to be social, like going out to eat or the movies...or dating, for that matter. Not that I wasn't terrified of dating. I had crushes on girls at school. I would've even liked to ask a few out, but I was so awkward. I didn't know how to do that. I was also a bit confused because my fantasies generally revolved around coaches, male teachers, and a few of my friends' fathers. I really didn't know what to make of it at the time. Like, I can spank it to one of my father's Playboys and then spank it thinking about kneeling in front of Coach Wayne.

The loophole for making money without having a job was mowing yards. Ironically, even though I'm not an outdoor person, I really enjoyed mowing yards. There's a certain Zen to it. There's a droning noise to block things out, but you have to focus just enough attention to follow the lines. It was also one of the few things I was good at. I could edge, weed eat, mow, clean up, and make a yard look really good. The pickup truck came in handy for this as well. So all through high school, during spring and summer, I would mow yards for cash. I would usually just stick to the weekends, but this limited the amount I could do.

I turned 18 last summer. I was a "man," now. Well, legally at least. This was my senior year, and I tried to be a little more assertive before going off to college next year. I decided that since my grades were pretty much locked, I would try to add to my routine to make some more money by doing some weekday evenings as well. That meant I would need to find more customers, so I ventured out in a broader radius to find them.

I rode around this one neighborhood, and I saw this yard in really rough shape. There were runners of grass growing over the curb and the driveway. The weeds by the edge of the fence and the yard looked like they didn't even get trimmed the year before. I figured I might try and make some extra cash. I'd hit the home-owner up for a bigger fee to get it looking right, but then I'd be able to keep it in shape the rest of the season without too much work, since it wasn't a huge or complicated yard to mow.

I walked to the front door, but a piece of paper was taped to it that said, "Use side door." I walked around to the carport and knocked on the door. I waited for what felt like forever, but was probably just over a minute. I knocked again since there was a car in the carport. I heard footsteps, and the door swung open quickly. The look on the man's face was like he was gonna gripe with maybe a snarly "what do you want?", but as soon as he saw me, his face changed to puzzled. I guess I wasn't who he expected to see at the door.

I, on the other hand, was completely caught off guard. The man didn't have on a shirt and was wearing only gray sweatpants. I tried to speak, but was com-pletely distracted looking at him. He was at least in his late 30s. He had quite a bit of a paunch, burgeoning on potbelly. His lower belly and chest were covered in light brown hair. His nipples were quite perky, slightly smaller than pencil erasers, with areolas bigger than a quarter. My mind wandered, thinking about sucking and nibbling on them. Nipples were (and still are) a par-ticular fixation of mine, along with body hair.

"Can I help you?" he asked.

I stammered, "I was wondering if, uh, you'd be in-terested in my yard mowing service?"

"That's funny," he said. His posture completely re-laxed. Like he was expecting a bill collector, and instead I was just some kid he didn't need to yell at.

He turned around and walked into his kitchen, leaving the door open with me peering in. I could see him rummaging through what looked like mail on the counter. I noticed a waistband peeking out the top of the sweatpants that looked like plaid boxers. He turned, bringing a piece of paper with him.

As he walked to me, I noticed a slight bulge in his grey sweatpants. I felt inferior about my cock size. I took every opportunity I could to check out a revealing bulge. I could just make out the outline of his head, and that he was clearly circumcised. It seemed a bit larger than mine. It wasn't dangling down a long way or anything, but it was noticeable, especially given the bit of belly he had. It was like the head was in front of his balls. Far more dangle than I had, as my soft cock often shriveled up. I could feel my tighty-whities starting to get a little tight in the front as I stared at it.

"Sorry about the way I opened the door. I expected you to be the city. I got this letter the other day." He showed me. It was about his yard not meeting community standards. I didn't read it closely, but I got the gist. "I mean, winter is barely over," he continued. "Although, who expected to jump right into a heatwave like this?" He pantomimed at the air outside. He wasn't wrong. Out of nowhere, we skipped spring; it was in the high 90s that day.

"How much do you charge?" he asked.

I started my pitch. "I've built a reputation on a quality job at a fair price. I charge $10 for a mow. You decide every week or every other, but I usually recommend every week with the type of grass you have. $15 when I weed eat, which I recommend once a month, but can do more often if you like. However, no disrespect, but your yard would require my startup fee to get it to a condition I can keep up for the mowing season. My father taught me that if I'm going to do a job, I'm going to do it right. My start fee is $40."

He shook his head. "That's a fair price for the mow. And your startup will get me out of an equal fine with the city if you can do it this week."

"I can do it today if you like."

He turned and went back to the counter. He looked in his wallet. "I've got enough on me. You have a deal."

"Great! I'm Charlie."

"Hi, Charlie. I'm Keith."

I learned long ago about protecting yourself while mowing (To this day, I have shrapnel in my shins from weed-eating wearing shorts). I always wore jeans and a long-sleeve t-shirt in case of poison ivy or thorns. I started by finding the edges of the driveway and curbs. I used a flat shovel to get all the runners back in the yard to chop up. I did the weed eater next and gave myself a wider-than-normal path since I don't know the yard well yet. As I put up the weed eater and got ready to mow, finally, the heat started really getting to me. As they say in the Deep South, "It's not the heat, it's the humidity." I decided it's safe enough to take my shirt off to mow, hoping I could cool off a little faster without the soaked shirt.

On my 2nd pass, something out of the corner of my eye caught my attention in the window. I didn't see anything, so I continued. A few passes later, I'm a bit closer to the house, and it happened again. This time, I could see the blinds swinging a bit. I thought maybe he was just checking on my work. Although my cock twitched at the thought that he might be watching me.

I finished up. I started loading my equipment in the bed of the truck. I heard the door open behind. I was still loading when I heard him say, "Man! It's never looked this good before. It's like yard of the month!" I turned around to smile and thank him, but mid-turn, I started to faint. I caught myself on the tailgate of the truck. I could feel myself flush, heat radiating from inside my body, different than a fever. He ran over to help catch me if I fell farther.

"Are you ok?" he asked.

"I'm overheated, I think," I choked out. "Got too caught up and forgot to drink enough water."

"What can I do to help?"

"Ice water. Need to cool down," I managed to say.

He helped me get under the shade of the carport. I sat on the step into his kitchen. He came back with a giant tumbler full of ice and water. I try to sip it slowly. I can tell I'm bright red.

"Let's get you in the air conditioning."

I didn't argue. I basically crawled up the single step with his help and collapsed on the kitchen linoleum. He refilled the glass. I drank it all. I could tell it wasn't helping. Apparently so could he.

"Should I call an ambulance?" he asked. His voice sounded concerned.

I shook my head. "Last time this happened, I just sat under a cold shower."

"Let's get you to the bathroom then."

He helped me off the floor and down the hall to his bathroom. He got me a towel out and set it on the sink. He turned just the cold knob on for me. "Shout if you need any help." He closed the door, leaving a crack, as he exited to give me privacy.

I struggled with my jeans, but they were so sweat-soaked and I was so weak that I couldn't get them off.

I eventually gave up and said as loudly as I could manage, "Mr. Keith! I'm stuck."

He cracked the door to hear better but didn't peer in. "Stuck?"

"I can't get my jeans off. Can you help me?"

He opened the door to see me on the ground. I had the back of the waist below my bottom. My bush was sticking out of the open fly, but the thighs were stuck. He grabbed the bottom of the legs by my heels, then turned his head away as he pulled. I wiggled and he tugged, and they eventually came off, my white briefs with them. He never looked back, just turning and carrying the jeans out of the room.

He said, "I'll hang these in the kitchen to hopefully dry a little," as he pulled the door behind him.

I crawled in the cold shower and sat under the water. I felt better within a few minutes as my body temperature started to drop.

He knocked on the door. "Are you alright?"

"It's starting to work."

"Good. Need anything?"

"More water, if that's not too much trouble?" I wasn't completely clear-headed yet, but I knew this was a major imposition to put a stranger and client in. I could hear my dad saying something about "unprofessional".

I heard his voice through the shower curtain. "Here you go."

I pulled back the curtain about a foot. We made brief eye contact before he looked away. I grabbed the tumbler, leaving the curtain open. As I took a long drink of ice water, the little devil inside wondered if I imagined that he looked down before he looked away.

I could see he's still looking away. I said, "I'm so sorry about this. Thank you for your kindness. This is above and beyond."

He instinctively turned to nod and say, "Thank you." He blushed a little. "It's really no problem. We've all overdone it before. Plus, you did such an amazing job on the yard. Really. It's never looked that good."

I was taking another long drink while he said this. I was looking just over the tumbler, hoping he thought I was looking in it and not at his crotch. I swore I saw his cock head move. I move my eyes up to his face. I just caught him looking at my crotch before meeting my eyes.

I was still delirious enough to say, "Can I ask you a personal question? You know, uh, man to man?"

He swallowed and kind of choke-coughed. "Maybe."

"I don't know why, but I feel I can be honest with you about something that would be embarrassing with my father or a teacher."

He nodded for me to continue.

"I always feel like my penis is small." I gestured at it with my open palm. My soft cock was just a head sitting on top of my balls. Although my balls weren't as tight as usual because of the heat. "I mean, it gets bigger when I get hard, but I've seen guys in the locker room dangling and flopping around, so I've just always had a complex about it. And not that I was looking," I wasn't sure if he could tell a difference in the red my face was turning now versus before, "but I kind of noticed your head hangs down at least in front of your balls." I was almost shocked that I'd let all that out, in nearly one breath, no less.

He paused. I began to worry I'd really fucked up with my verbal diarrhea.

"Son," he smiled, "we all go through that around your age. And there's nothing to be worried about. Penises come in a variety of shapes and sizes. What you're describing about yourself is known as a grower. One that looks tiny when soft, but I'll bet it looks normal when hard. Some guys have danglers. They may hang several inches long when soft, but often don't grow much more in length when hard. We call those show-ers. I'm a bit of both. A grower and a show-er. I have a little length when soft, but still get a little bigger when hard."

My eyes were fixated on his crotch. I was watching his cock slowly move. It was still pointing downward, but the head had moved downward at least 2 inches.

"Everyone thinks the big ones are something to be jealous of, but I'm sure the average and the small ones have just as much enjoyment when stimulated."

His cock started to move away from his body just a little.

He stopped talking. I looked up slack-jawed. Our eyes met. I swallowed.

You don't have anything to worry about. You look

perfectly average to me, from what I can see," he nodded down in the direction of my crotch.

I looked down. I was fully erect. My cock stood poking outward and slightly up.

"Have you ever measured yours?" I asked.

"Sure. I think most men do at some point."

"Mine's 5 and a half inches long and 5 inches around," I blurt out.

"See. Right in the middle of average." He gave me a reassuring smile.

I nodded thanks. Then, I gave him a look, hoping he would share.

He reluctantly added, "Mine's a little longer and just a little less girthy than what you described."

I looked down a bit, sheepishly. "Would it be weird if I wanted to see it?"

"Oh, I don't know if that would be appropriate. I could get in a lot of trouble. How old are you?"

"I turned 18 last summer." I had an implied "please" in my voice.

He looked nervous.

"I won't tell anyone. I promise. I'm just curious. And you're so easy to talk to about it."

"Well," he said nervously. "Just a peek. Full disclosure. I'm not hard, but I'm not completely soft either."

I nodded, excited.

He pulled down both sweatpants and boxers at the same time. He stopped about mid-thigh.

I gasped. I shuffled onto my knees, kneeling in the tub, but just leaning to the edge of the tub for a better look.

It was soft, but just hard enough to have a consistent downward curve and lifting away from his balls. It was a little over 6 inches already, which meant what I saw earlier in his pants was likely 4-5 soft. It was slimmer than mine. Then I noticed his balls. They were huge, and his sack sagged, letting them dangle greatly with any little movement he made.

"Whoa," I said softly. "It's not fully hard and bigger than mine. And I didn't know balls could be that big. You must shoot a big load."

"I do," he beamed with pride.

I looked up at him, my eyes wide. He laughed at my obviously being impressed. I looked back down and swore it had grown a bit more.

"I get some distance, too," he added.

"I shot on my chest lying down once," I bragged.

"I usually hit the wall above my headboard."

I quickly looked at his face to see if he was pulling my leg. He nodded with an earnest look. I could tell it was the truth, and the look on my face changed from disbelief to amazement. He laughed harder this time. I looked back down to watch his belly jiggle, his balls sway, and his cock bounce. As he laughed, I don't know why, but I couldn't control myself and I reached out and grabbed his cock underhanded - resting in my palm. He startled as my hand made contact, but he didn't pull away. I just held it. It felt heavier than mine in my hand. I lightly bounced it to test the weight. I gently squeezed it. He closed his eyes and gently tilted his head back.

His cock continued to grow as I handled it. I was mesmerized by the weight and texture, having only ever felt my own. A vein on top started to become visible, slightly blue. I took my other hand and cupped his hefty balls. He moaned lightly. They didn't fit in my palm. Unlike my tight sack, his hung enough that you could wrap your fingers around the top. My fingers barely touched. I did it instinctively and started to tug them. He moaned again. I let go of his cock and rubbed his belly while I tugged his balls. It was perfect. Everything I thought that made a man a man, a nice belly, body hair, and a big dick...well bigger than mine. I was envious and also wanted to worship his body at the same time.

I suddenly realized that he was at full mast now. It

was a big one, by my standards. I was sure he had an inch and a half on me, making him 7 inches. Perfectly straight, not a curve to it. The vein on top really popped out now. And he was right, it felt just a little slimmer than mine in my hand.

I leaned forward, opening my mouth as I did. I took the head in my mouth and began to suck. He gasped. I worked more and more in and out of my mouth. I got about halfway down his shaft, and he lightly held my head, running his fingers through my hair. I could hear him mumbling, "This is wrong. This is wrong." But he made no move to stop me. I got a bit more in my mouth, and he began to thrust slightly. I could taste precum and needed to swallow. As I did, the swallow motion got a big growl out of him. He grabbed my head firmer and started to thrust more. Harder and deeper he went until he eventually hit the back of my throat and gagged.

It was like he'd been in a trance and snapped out of it. "I'm sorry. I'm so sorry. We shouldn't be doing this."

I drank some water to help with the coughing from gagging. I hoarsely said, "No. I like it."

"You're turning blue in that cold shower. Let's get you out."

He handed me a towel. I dried off. Rock hard the whole time. He was as well. But he pulled his pants up.

I said, "Thank you. I'm sorry if I overstepped."

"We're all curious about different things," he offered.

I was done drying. "Should I get dressed now?" My cock strained at the need for release.

"Well, your clothes are still probably quite wet. We could lay down a bit to see if they dry a bit more."

I nodded, a little too excited.

He led me to his bedroom. I could see a few cum stains on the wall above. I pointed and smiled. He just nodded and shrugged, smirking.

I asked, "How many times a day do you get off?"

"3 if I get to come home at lunch. Sometimes 4 on the weekend. You?"

"I've done 3 once, but it was a lot of work. Twice a day if there's a long break in between. But it does get hard again right away. Just can't squirt again for at least a few hours."

He just laughed. He motioned for me to lie on the bed. "Least I can do is return the favor." He got between my legs. Just as he was about to put my cock in his mouth, he asked, "Have you ever done anything like this before?"

I shook my head. "Just me and my hand."

"Are you sure you're ok with this?"

"I don't know. But I'm not nervous, so I'm following that instinct."

"Close your eyes."

I felt his warm breath as his wide mouth engulfed my cock before sealing his lips around it. His first suck sent me writhing on the bed. His tongue was everywhere, but his head moved slowly. I don't think I lasted even 30 seconds. It felt like the most spunk I'd ever shot in my life. I'd never had so many quakes while cumming.

I couldn't move for a while. I was spent from such an intense orgasm. I could feel him licking every drop that leaked out of my slit. When I finally opened my eyes, he was looking up at me, still between my legs. "Quite a load. Very tasty."

I sat up, and he sat on the bed next to me. "I never imagined it could be so intense. I'm a little disappointed I didn't last longer."

"We all shoot quickly the first time."

"My turn!" I quickly jumped over between his legs, grabbing both his waistbands. He waddled in place to let me get them down. Once I had them off, he scooched up on the bed, and I got between his legs.

He was still rock hard, his head slick with precum. I dove onto his cock. I tried to emulate everything I felt when he sucked me. Tongue and head movements. I worked his balls again. Every new thing I did got an approving moan. I kept one hand on his balls and reached up to finally play with his nipples. As I began to play with one, my spent cock started to twitch. As it got harder, my horniness made me take more shaft in my mouth. I knew my limit now, but I stayed right at the threshold of it.

His balls began to tighten. He grabbed my head again and began to thrust. I could tell he was trying not to choke me. He held me farther up the shaft this time.

A low moan started from him. It grew louder and louder until he suddenly held still and held my head in place. That first volley had such force I almost choked as it pelted the back of my throat. He shot rope after rope of thick cum in my mouth. I lost count of the number of spasms I felt pulse through his cock. I had to try to swallow at least 4 times before he stopped cumming.

He was lying on the bed with his heading tilted down, looking at me.

"Wow," he said. "You didn't spill a drop. I'm proud of you."

I beamed a giant smile.

"You're quite a natural," he said, causing me to blush. "You sure you've never done that before?"

"I just tried to copy what you did to me. It felt incredible."

"You had some good moves in the bathroom before I even got a taste of yours," he winked at me.

I just shrugged and blushed more.

I decided I'd lie beside him. As I got up, he said, "Boy, you weren't kidding! Looks like you're ready to go again."

I looked down at my boner, standing straight out. "I guess I really enjoyed that."

"Oh, really? Sucking my cock and swallowing my big load got you horned up again that quick, huh?"

I nodded as I lay down beside him. I nestled in his arm, laying my head on his chest. He closed his eyes, still catching his breath. I began to lap at his nipple with the tip of my tongue. I could feel precum leaking from my boner as it rubbed against his thigh as I licked. He didn't seem to mind, so I adjusted my position so I could suckle and nibble his perky nip. I rubbed his ample belly. My cock responded even more. I lightly humped his now slick leg. My cock ached for release again, as if I hadn't just emptied my balls minutes before.

"Damn. You're a horny little fucker, aren't you?" He didn't even open his eyes.

I stopped. I looked at his face, his eyes still closed. I wasn't sure from his tone if I should keep going. I mustered up some courage and said, "I think it's just you, Mr. Keith. Everything about you just gets me going."

"You can just call me Keith, son," he said gently. He turned his head while opening his eyes and looked right into mine. "Or you can call me Sir, if you'd like." My cock jumped. I even felt my nipples harden. I didn't understand why, but the way he said it took hold over me."

"Yes, sir," I said with a head nod in the most serious voice I could manage.

He started to sit up. "Since you're raring to go, you want me to show some other things?"

I just nodded as emphatically as I could. He was standing on his knees on the bed. He used one hand to grab my hip and start to roll me over. "Get on all fours," he said.

My face must have looked scared, because he chuckled and added, "I'm all about pleasure, not pain. I won't hurt you." I nodded and got up on all fours like he asked. "If that gets uncomfortable, you can drop your upper body down. Like laying your head down on a desk."

"Ok," I replied, not knowing what to expect.

"Now, since you had the shower to cool off, you should be clean already."

I wasn't sure what he meant. He grabbed my butt cheeks and spread them apart. I jumped as something warm and wet touched my butthole. He pulled me back by the hips. The tip of his tongue wet my hole again. It was an alien sensation. He alternated between swirling around, licking up and down, then side to side. Just the tip tickling. I moaned. I didn't mean to. It just happened. He changed to the full width of his tongue, licking up, like an ice cream cone. I moaned again, louder, without thinking. He'd vary to moves I could only guess at, each a new sensation. I folded my arms and lay my head and chest on the bed, my legs keeping my ass up. His tongue, tightened to a point, jabbed at my puckering rosette. I could feel my hole pulsing as his tongue assaulted it, all while giving me intense pleasure. I was making noises that could have been from a wild animal. I was in a daze when he grabbed my cock, snapping me out of it. It was slick with precum. He stroked it only twice before letting go, making me writhe. "Damn, boy. You love it when I rim you, huh?"

I managed a weak, "Ye-Yes, sir."

"That pink pucker of yours is begging for it." He jabbed his tongue again, then twirled in a circle. I felt his lips seal around my pucker, and he sucked my hole. I thought my legs would collapse. He would alternate between those 2 moves. It felt like his tongue was making its way into my hole. It was ecstasy.

He stopped. I could tell he moved to reach around me, rummaging on his bedside table. "You're starting to loosen up real good. I'm getting some lube. I'm gonna stick a finger in there and teach you about the male g-spot."

I felt him spread something cool and very slick on my hole. I felt just a little pressure as the tip of his finger slipped into my hole. I let out a little moan, deeper than before. "Yeah," he said gently. "That's a good boy. Just to my first knuckle. Gonna spread the lube around." I could feel him twist his finger, getting the lube on all sides. He pulled his finger out. "I'm gonna squirt a little inside. It might feel weird." I nodded as best I could and mumbled "Um-hmm." The bottle had a little cone tip. He gently pushed it, much smaller than his finger had been. I felt a squirt of cold liquid inside me, and then oozing down my balls as he pulled it out while squeezing. His fingertip slipped in with no resistance this time. He continued to slowly push it in. He moaned this time. "Damn, son. You really loosened up from my eating that sweet ass of yours. My finger's going all the way in." Just as he got his finger in as far as he could, he grazed something inside me. I gasped in pleasure. "Ye-heah," laughed. "That feels good, doesn't it?"

I mumbled noise.

"I'm gonna put my middle finger in so I can reach it better." I heard him put some lube on his middle finger. It was thicker, and my hole stretched a little as he slid it in. Not completely unpleasant, but he wasn't taking his time this time. Then his finger hit the spot again and kept going past it. I didn't think about my hole any-more, just the blinding sensations. He rubbed it, pulling his finger in and out, occasionally stopping in the middle to rub left and right or just press and wiggle. I was lost in a sea of bliss. I could hear him through the haze in my mind, "This is your prostate. Your hole can give you a lot of pleasure, but your prostate is a whole other level." He continued to finger me, taking longer strokes in and out. He added more lube when he sensed my hole needed it.

I don't know how long this went on, but eventually, he pulled out completely and squirted more lube in me. I felt my hole stretch. "Deep breath in and hold. Now relax as you slowly exhale. Keep repeating that." I did as I was told. My hole stretched more and more. It was pleasurable and unpleasant at the same time. I would wench, and he would hold and twist until it relaxed a bit more. He would use his other hand to stroke my hole to help it relax as I continued to breathe. He eventually got to my prostate again. As soon as he touched it, my hole opened right up. "That's a good boy," he said. His voice was breathy and lustful. "That's 2 fingers all the way in." He panted. "Goddamn, I'm rock hard again."

He pulled his fingers out. I felt the bed move. I felt something blunt rubbing up and down against my hole. It felt good. Rubbing my hole, letting it recover a bit. I thought it might be a thumb, but I wasn't sure. He whispered loud enough I could hear it, "You've got me leaking like a faucet. I don't want it to go to waste, son. I'm rubbing it on your hole." It was his cock rubbing my hole. I let out a little, "Ohhhh," at the thought of it. He stopped rubbing it and just left it, applying pressure on my hole. It felt wonderful after that 2-finger stretch. Just gentle pressure. I felt his precum oozing down my taint. I moaned at the thought of it, relaxing and pushing back without thinking about it. His head popped right into my hole. I whimpered as it did. I could see stars from the pain.

I took a big gasp. He stood perfectly still, rubbing the small of my back. "Just relax. Let it adjust." The pain soon started to dissipate, replaced by a stretch to my hole that was indescribable in its pleasure while at the threshold of uncomfortable. He could tell I was adjusting to it and started to slide in, pulling my hips. He took his time, moaning most of the way. The pressure as his head passed my G-spot was more intense than his finger had been. He continued slowly pushing until I felt the hairs on his balls tickle my taint. He inhaled deeply through his nose. "This little cherry of yours is tighter than I could have imagined. Whew. You doing ok, son?"

"Um-hmm," I managed.

He pulled out slowly, about halfway, and then back

in. He kept this rhythm for a few strokes until I started to moan again.

'Yeah, you like that dick in you, boy?"

I could barely, "Um-hmm." again.

He picked up the pace. "I bet you do. You like getting fucked, don't you? Answer me, boy."

"Yes, sir," I said.

"Fuck yeah, you do." Pounding me harder and faster. "You want me cum deep inside you?"

"Yes, sir." I almost yelled this time. I wanted to reach down and jerk off, knowing I'd cum within a few strokes, but I couldn't reach.

"Your hole is just too tight. I'm gonna cum too soon." He let out a growl and pulled my hips, thrusting his cock as deep as it would go. I felt spurt after spurt of cum fill my bowels. I felt his shaft pulse against my prostate. I felt the spasm lessen, and his cock began to soften still inside me. He collapsed on the bed as he pulled out of me.

I lay on my side, looking at him, breathing deeply. I fiddled with my cock, aching for release. It was covered in so much precum that it made noises like the lube in my hole had. He opened his eyes, looking down at me, stroking. "You poor thing. Let me help with that. He got down between my legs. He began to suck my cock. He easily slipped 2 fingers in my loose, sloppy hole, using his cum as additional lube.

I writhed for 20 minutes as he stimulated every nerve in my cock, balls, and ass. He'd get me right to the edge and then change his technique, keeping me from the climax I desired.

"Sir," I finally begged, "I need cum. Please make me cum. I can't take it anymore."

He looked up and smiled at me with a devilish grin. "You'll thank me for all that teasing when you finally pop," winking at me after he said it.

He stood, grabbed the bottle of lube, bent over the bed, and squirted some in his hole. He reached back, rubbing the excess on his hole. He turned his head toward me and said, "Give it to me, boy. Give me everything you've got. I can take it. Take my hole the way I took your cherry."

My eyes were wild. "Yes, sir," I said in a low, gravelly voice, almost vindictive. I was so pent up, my horniness was completely in control, determined to get release. I stood behind him and lined my cockhead up with his slick hole. I grabbed his hips and shoved all the way. He whelped in surprise. "Yeah, boy," he yelled, "Use my hole like I did yours." I thrust as fast and as hard as I could. I was determined to spunk inside him. "Oh fuck, son. Fuck me hard like that. Abuse my hole."

"Yes, sir," I replied gruffly, "I'm gonna fuck this hole as long as I can. I'm gonna wear your hole out til you beg for mercy," nearly screaming at the end." "Oh, yes," he whimpered, "Make me pay. You're tearing up my poor hole." I pounded hard strokes all the way in. I started pulling all the way out and slamming all the way in. "Oh, yes," he yelled, "tear me apart, son."

I pulled out. I don't know how, but I flipped him on his back. I pushed his knees towards his chest. I slammed my cock back into him. He cried out, then whimpered as I pounded. I could feel at this angle, my head was jabbing his prostate every pass I made. His cock was still limp from fucking me, but it oozed fresh, clear precum. His eyes glazed over. I could tell this was what my face had looked like as he'd played with my hole in various ways. He was lost in ecstasy now.

"Is this what you like, 'Sir'?" I spat the words at him, "For your boy to fuck you senseless?" He looked me in the eye and just nodded as I continued to fuck him as hard and fast as I could. I put his legs over my shoulders to free my hands. I rubbed the precum he was oozing onto his belly. My balls began to tighten. I grabbed a nipple in each hand, flicking and gently twisting and pulling at first. He began to writhe, wiggling his bottom, causing us the grind together as I fucked into him. The harder I worked his nipples, the more he moved, and the tighter my balls got. I loved working his nipples. I could feel they were part of the key to my release. I began to squeeze and twist harder. Still making eye contact, his jaw dropped as he began to gasp, "Oh, god. Oh, god. Oh, god. I'm gonna cum. Milk me, boy! Milk it."

His cock was still limp, but a 3rd huge load for the day came oozing, instead of shooting out all over his bush. His hole clamped onto my shaft with each pulse as my cock forced an orgasm out of his prostate. I squeezed his nips as hard as I could and thrust all the way in. His spasming hole sent me over the edge. I'd never shot a load that big or that intense. It was so much cum, it was shooting out of his hole around my cock. I lost count of the number of spurts, but more than a dozen. I collapsed on the bed, my cock slipping out of his hole, much like he'd earlier.

He turned to me and smirked, "I told you it would be worth all the edging." I smiled back as I passed out from exhaustion.

I woke, not knowing where I was. I was naked but had been cleaned up a bit as I wasn't covered in cum and lube. I touched my hole. It was a little tender but felt as normal as I could remember. Not that I'd ever messed with it much.

I walked out front. My clothes were in the kitchen. They weren't dry, but they were dry enough to put on to go home. Just as I finished getting them on, Keith came back in through the door. "You really did a great job on the yard. The neighbors are all asking if you're looking for other customers."

"Sure," I said, smiling. He handed me $50. "This is too much."

"That's a tip...for the yard," he clarified to make sure I didn't think it was for something else.

"Thank you," I said.

"Did you have a good time?"

"Yes...Sir," I half winked after the pause as I said it.

He adjusted his cock. "Only when we play. Otherwise, you'll get me started again."

We both laughed.

He added, raising his eyebrows, "But I might have to call you 'Sir' sometimes. I think I liked being punished for being naughty."

Poolside Plantings

PETER SCHUTES

L os Angeles was 100 miles away, but it might as well have been 10,000 miles. I was finally relaxed. Someone in the hot tub commented that I had a nice smile. I don't think I'd smiled for years.

After endless years on contract at MGM, I was finally able to take a vacation. The contract expired. I had saved enough to live for a few years if I chose not to work again. This trip to Palm Springs was quite literally what the doctor ordered. My blood pressure was through the roof. I was starved of vitamin D. Basking in the sunshine in my Speedo, I could feel my skin drinking in the light. That's when I saw Bailey.

The clothing-optional resort catered only to men. The owner was queer, as were all his clientele. Nobody was required to wear clothing. This meant that the employees of the resort had to be comfortable working around a bunch of naked gay men. Bailey was the new groundskeeper. He was so good-looking, he had to dress ugly on purpose. He was over six feet tall, with dirty blonde hair. He wore coke bottle glasses and a thick mustache, hiding his handsome face. Every time he moved, his muscles threatened to burst through the fabric of his clothes. I was surrounded by a crowd of mostly naked men, but all I saw was Bailey, bending to pick up a pot of geraniums. Even from behind, I could see the outline of his cock running down the inside of the left leg of his jeans.

I'm a bottom by design, not by choice. My fat cock looks good in a swimsuit. It attracts a lot of curious men, anxious to take a ride. Once it comes out of the swimsuit and swells to full size, they walk away. Unless they're very experienced, they know they can't do a thing. If I'm lucky, they're versatile, and I get a good ass fucking. In Los Angeles, they're usually 100% bottom with zero interest in giving me the pleasure they'd hoped to reap from me.

Bailey didn't seem to notice my huge bulge. He kept at his job, patiently planting pansies and geraniums in terra cotta pots. I had to walk past him to get to my room, and I needed to pee. With my fat cock crammed into my Speedo, I wiggled and walked to my room. I nodded at Bailey and said, "Hi."

Bailey looked up, pushed his thick glasses to his forehead, and smiled. "Hey, man." His voice was deep. It made me shiver.

He went back to planting. I took a piss in the room and stuffed everything back carefully, to hide as much as I could. I know very little about gardening, but I do know that geraniums are perennials in Los Angeles. Palm Springs has different weather. He was right outside my door, potting geraniums.

"I thought geraniums were perennials."

Bailey looked up with a serious expression. "Not in the Springs. By August these'll be crispy." He stood and wiped his hands on his jeans before extending one.

"Bailey."

I took his meaty palm in mine. It was cracked and rough. "Peter."

We stood silently for what felt like an eternity, but was most likely about ten seconds. Bailey licked his lips.

"We ain't allowed in the guest's rooms."

"Are we allowed in yours?"

When he was done planting for the day, Bailey stowed away the wheelbarrow and tools. I was lying by the pool, my fat, throbbing meat wrapped in spandex. I saw silent whispers between guests, some of whom stared unabashedly at my hard-on. Every time Bailey bent to put away a tool, I got harder. I didn't know what would happen between us, but I knew I was going to like it. Bailey closed up the garden shed and padlocked it.

He whispered. "I'm in 46. Wait five minutes." Bailey walked with a bit of a limp. I could see his massive cock trapped in his jeans. I suppose the rest of the resort could see it too. It was impossible to miss, just like mine.

Before I could knock, Bailey whisked me inside. He planted his lips on mine, his tongue gently exploring my mouth. I pushed back, tasting his toffee-scented breath. I put a hand on his inner thigh, rubbing the long log of flesh that throbbed and strained against the denim. He reciprocated, caressing my cock through the strained fabric of my swimsuit until it stuck out like a tent pole. It was thick as a beer can.

Bailey knelt and freed my fatty from its prison. His big hands held it. The fingers couldn't touch. He buried his lips in my foreskin and tongued the tip. I'm a shower and a grower. It got bigger. His eyes widened. I waited for the familiar rejection.

"You're like me!" He stood. After getting the waist past his protruding ass, he lowered his jeans to his knees to free the monster. It lifted to a 90-degree angle, poking my belly button. His cock was longer than mine, but it was the same size around, like two soup cans stacked on each other. Bailey held me close. My cock went between his legs, while his pressed to his chest, rising past the nipple line. I only needed to lower my head to lick the tip. He shivered.

I said, "Bailey, I've never been with someone as big as you. I'm not sure I can take it."

He grinned. "Me neither." I wasn't sure if he meant he didn't know if he could take me or if I could take him. Turned out it was both.

Bailey said, "Pete, you wanna try fucking me?" I hadn't fucked anyone since high school. I was just too big. Yes, I wanted to try fucking him. But I knew it was hopeless. Still, I nodded.

"I gotta prepare." He went to the bathroom. The door was open; I saw him in the mirror. He douched, then he took some diet pills out of the cabinet and crushed them with a glass. He caught my eye in the mirror.

"You want some? It makes it easier." He snorted some with a short straw. I took the straw and inhaled the bitter powder. At first, I felt nothing. Then I heard a ringing in my ears. My cock got so hard I thought it would explode.

Bailey climbed up on the bed, wriggling his muscled ass. I licked the musky hole. The scent drove me wild. I lapped and sucked and licked, forcing my tongue deeper into his hole. It was surprisingly loose. His cock hung down like an udder. I milked it while I sucked, stretching his balls until the tip of his cock leaked pre-cum. I caught the pre-cum on my tongue and licked his hole, tasting the salty dribble as it worked its way into his hole.

Bailey moaned. "Oh, Peter. Fuck me. Fuck me." He handed me a jar of Albolene. I slicked up my cock with the grease and spit on it. I spat in my greasy hand a few times and wiped Bailey's hole with the mixture.

"You ready?"

He nodded. He picked up a little glass vial and popped it, inhaling the fumes. He handed it to me. I inhaled, and my whole world throbbed. I knelt over Bailey, who lay prostrate on his mattress. I lined my cock head up with his hole. Letting gravity do some of the work, I pushed until the very tip of my cock entered the warm hole. Bailey popped another vial.

"Quick! Now!"

I watched my cock head as his hole swallowed it up. I could swear he was pulling me inside him. Once the head was in, the rest of the fuck was a straight shot. My hips pressed against his round buttocks. I was inside a man for the first time in years. I nearly cried.

I was so surprised and excited, I wasn't able to hold back for very long. Twenty or thirty good strokes, and I shot my load up inside him. I pulled out my dripping cock, wiping the excess cum on his backside. I marveled at the way his hole stayed open, like a recently-caught fish gasping for oxygen on the pier.

Bailey rolled over and smiled. "Your turn."

I didn't think I could take it. I'd been fucked three ways to Sunday but never by a man as big and thick as Bailey. He used greasy fingers to stretch my hole. I felt him press against my prostate and jumped. He fingered me there again and again, watching me thrash with ecstasy.

As much as it took me to grease up my own pole, it was nothing to the amount of Albolene that Bailey needed to lube up his. He spat over and over, polishing his huge cock until it shone. He flipped me onto my back, holding my legs on his shoulders, and handed me another glass ampoule.

I popped the glass, and just as I began inhaling, I felt blinding pain in my nether regions. The poppers made my muscles relax, but they didn't take away the pain. Bailey forced himself halfway in, until his cock rammed against the end of my rectum. He leaned over and kissed me. He pushed hard as he lifted my left side close to him. Suddenly, his cock popped through an opening I knew well. He was in my colon now. He held the poppers to my nose and pushed again. With a loud smack, his hips hit my butt.

I recognized the tears of joy in his eyes. He probably hadn't been inside anyone either. I lifted my head, watching in fascination as the huge cock slid in and out of me. Bailey's rhythm became a locomotive, speeding up with each stroke until he was a jackhammer.

"Oh fuck! Jesus Christ! Fucking fuck!" My eyes rolled into my head. I couldn't see, only feel. It was terrible pain mixed with a pleasure so sublime, it was worth any amount of pain. I felt completely filled with flesh on the in-stroke, and terribly empty on the out-stroke. Over and over, he pounded me until I lost the power of speech. I moaned softly. Bailey kissed me, holding my shoulders against the bed so he could fuck even harder.

"I'm gonna plant my seed in you." It was funny, coming from a gardener. I nodded weakly.

He threw his head back and gave a quiet shout. I felt a warm flood fill my insides. As Bailey fucked, filling my lower digestive tract, there was nowhere for the cum to go. It shot past his cock, out of my hole, staining the bed. He collapsed on top of me. I held his muscular ass, marveling how it had accepted my fat cock just minutes earlier. Next, it was the powerhouse that drove his violent thrusts.

The diet pills were doing their job. I was rock hard, throbbing against Bailey's belly button. He winked.

"Something's up, eh?"

I nodded.

"I think we'll have a whole garden planted by the end of the night." He was right.

THE MOST DANGEROUS FLOWER

BY J. W. STEED

Mr. Carr of the Campbell

❧

Four months it's been since I re-entered the dating pool. Sixteen weeks, more or less, of pointless chit-chat over dubious arugula lunch salads. One hundred and twenty days of downloading and discarding apps, of agonizing over which way to swipe. Hell, a quarter-year of trying to figure out how to take a half-decent selfie—a skill all the kids these days have mastered. And by kids, I mean anyone under the age of forty.

None of my efforts has borne fruit. Half the men I meet seem uninterested until I mention I occupy a floor at The Campbell, one of Manhattan's landmark residences. The other half don't know what The Campbell is. Which is worse: the guy who dates me for my address, or the one who doesn't recognize it?

I know who's the absolute worst: me, for finding fault in every potential date. Perhaps after thirty years with my late husband Kenneth, all of them exclusive save for one slip-up, I'm not anxious to land myself another relationship. I've barely gotten over losing one.

Last week, I'd even returned to the Townhouse, where I'd met Kenneth a lifetime ago. Maybe, I thought, history might repeat itself: someone younger, hungrier, and beautiful might wander in and catch my eye, then spend his next thirty years with me. Three decades in the past, I'd been that scrawny little punk with nowhere to sleep, who had spent the last of his dough on a headful of terrible frosted tips. One cold winter night in the early nineties, I'd struck up a conversation with a well-dressed older gentleman at the Townhouse's piano bar.

"You've got potential," he'd said, looking me over. Maybe he admired my sheer nerve, walking into what I thought was Manhattan's ritziest gay establishment while sporting a horrifying dye job. "Are you a hustler, kid?"

I'd shaken my head. No, sir. I was not. Although I'd stumbled into this bar in the East Fifties willing to barter my ass for a little flow, technically I hadn't swapped sex for cash. Not yet.

Kenneth took me to his home in The Campbell that night. I'd never left.

Thank God he'd set me up for life, long before we both saw the end coming. His trust had been rock-solid; the will airtight. We had married as soon as it was legal. The two greedy brothers who'd shunned him in life had crept out from under their rocks the moment the obituary hit the papers, sniffing around. Kenneth's lawyers shooed them back to Bumfuck, PA, post-haste.

Though we hadn't been sexual in the last...ten? fifteen?...years of our relationship, I owed everything to Kenneth Kleinsmith. I had been his boy for over half my life. But the world has changed since that night long ago, when I first dropped my backpack onto the Italian mosaics of The Campbell's greenhouse suite.

After three decades, I no longer trust my instincts. They usually go sideways, quickly.

Case in point: my cab has just let me out in front of The Campbell. I'm about to walk up from Central Park West to its entrance when from the mahogany and glass doors bursts a guy who looks like trouble. Scowling, thick eyebrows. Dark eyes like a brewing storm. Darker masses of long, wavy hair in breathtaking disorder, tamped down by a pair of over-the-ear headphones. A week's worth of stubble covers his sculpted cheeks. He's young—no more than twenty-nine or thirty, wearing nothing more than a grimy white tee with a V-neck worn and stretched into a W-neck. His hands thrust deep in the pockets of his oversized dungarees, which sport hems so frayed the threads fringe his boots and trail across the sidewalk.

And oh, good lord, how badly I want him. I shouldn't. But I do.

None of the polite, well-dressed men with whom I've shared meals these last four months stirred my libido. Not one of the hopefuls at the Townhouse raised my internal temperature. The mere sight of this dirty stranger, though, clobbers me like a sack of bricks. I'm so overwhelmed with...well, with something I haven't felt in years...that I freeze, gawping, as he stomps past.

In seeming slow motion, he raises an arm to arrest the cab I've vacated. My head lolls to the side as I survey a rippling display of muscles in the forearms and biceps alone, punctuated by a peek at the thick dark hair springing from beneath his armpit. Whorls of dark ink cover his other arm; he's tattooed from wrist to shoulder. A sleeve, I think the kids call it. Though I'm in decent shape for a man my age, my muscle boy days are sadly in my past—and Kenneth always preferred me lean, not built. But I know how much effort has gone into transforming this stranger into a vision of sinew and steel.

Time flows like cold molasses. His dark, suspicious eyes slide in my direction as he passes. I wonder what he must see from their cat-like corners: a tall, spare-framed old man in his fifties, possibly having a stroke and definitely drooling from one side of his mouth as he stares and hangs onto the open cab door. My calfskin Beam tote drops to the bricks. I'm dressed head to toe in beige Loro Piana, the dullest and blandest camouflage of the well-to-do, as boring as it is expensive. Yet, as he passes, I feel foppish.

I cannot imagine what business he might have at The Campbell. This rough-hewn vision of masculinity certainly doesn't live here. Other residences might buckle to tax breaks by accommodating low-income housing, but beyond our marble arch, there's none of that nonsense. The Campbell's board blackballs actors as too vulgar. Even those with multiple Oscars.

"Thanks, dude." His address arrives as a chesty growl. Has he assumed I'm holding the cab for him? Ordinarily, I'd be outraged at the sheer cheek. But as he pours himself into the back seat and snarls out a Harlem address, all I can do is shut the door and stare wordlessly until his ride turns a corner and vanishes from sight. Only then do I sigh and pick up my bag from the pavement.

He didn't see me, of course. No one sees me. Still, I've never wanted anyone more in my life. When was the last time my insides had liquified like this? Forever ago, when I was younger and more feral.

Decades with Kenneth have over-civilized me. Not much to do about it, now.

I lope through the front doors of The Campbell and at once find myself fussed over by Luis, our shortest and most rotund doorman. "Mister Carr!" He attempts to relieve me of my tote. For a moment, I worry he might stand on tiptoes to fix my windblown hair.

"I'm good. Thank you, Luis," I assure him, as drunkenly I stumble across the palazzo tile. Is it possible to become intoxicated by a stranger's pheromones? Such a brief encounter, yet the world whirls around me as if I've been on a bender.

"Mister Carr! Are you all right, Mister Carr?"

Months ago, I would have corrected Luis and insisted he employ my first name. In the early years, doormen referred to me as *Mr. Kleinsmith's friend*. Once it became obvious that I wasn't going anywhere, *Johnny.*

I didn't dare query what they called me behind my back. Ever since the day Kenneth's estate went into probate, though, I've been *Mister Carr* to all the staff. I miss the informality from the days when they'd seen me as the kept boy, the accessory to the man with the money—at least then they considered me another employee on the payroll. Almost a comrade in arms.

Now I'm the man with the money. With it comes being treated as if I'm helpless. "I'm good," I assure Luis, waggling the calfskin bag to assure him I can handle its weight. I've just returned from a board meeting for one of my charities, which these days distributes minutes and handouts digitally to our devices. I may be the only relic who still believes in fine accessories. "Are there any, ah...?"

He notices my glance toward the wall of ornate mailboxes. "Miss Helga collected your mail before she left for the evening, sir. Mister Carr..."

"That was good of her." Balance regained, I clear my mind of any lingering thoughts of the man with whom I had crossed paths, outside. "Thank you, Luis."

"Mister Carr!" I detect a note of impatience in Luis' voice. He's been trying to tell me something. "Miss Helga tells me you're planning to get rid of Mr. Kleinsmith's orchids."

Oh. Yes. News travels fast. That very morning, I'd asked the housekeeper to arrange for someone to clean out the two greenhouses. *Burn it all. I don't care*, had been my exact words.

I stare blankly at the doorman, unprepared for his reproach. "Mr. Kleinsmith loved those orchids, sir."

I toy with my wedding ring, looking anywhere but at the attendant in his maroon uniform with the traditional gold chains. "Yes. He did."

"The orchids are the pride of The Campbell." Luis digs in deeper, making me uncomfortable. "How many magazines have they appeared in? My wife remembers seeing them on Regis and Kathie Lee!"

Abstracted and staring, I try to calculate how many years back that must have been. But that's how long the greenhouse has been The Campbell's boast. Kenneth had loved those flowers.

I open my mouth to explain, to justify, but the doorman talks on. "I know you have much to do, so if the orchids are a problem, I have a nephew. He's a good boy. A hard worker. He knows plants. He's studying for a degree..."

"Fine." With a single word, I commute the sentence of the damned orchids. "When can he come take a look?" I picture the plant kid as a miniature version of his uncle—a roly-poly Brazilian with spectacles and a squint. A bit of a nerd, but good with a watering can.

"Tomorrow? In the morning?"

"Tomorrow morning it is." Stepping into the elevator, I punch the button for the greenhouse suite. "Ten o'clock. I prefer punctuality."

"Oh, he will be right on time, Mister Carr! You won't regret it, I promise!" Apparently, I'm considered too feeble to insert my key into the hole by my button, as Luis does it for me with his master. The doors slide mercifully shut, but I still hear him calling, as I begin to ascend, "Ten o'clock on the dot!"

The Botanist

❧

Kenneth's orchids are, in fact, a problem. Hundreds of them occupy the suite's two Art Deco greenhouses, one at each end. Those half domes of glass and patinaed copper are The Campbell's most striking feature, visible from Central Park West below. The orchids themselves were famous before I became Kenneth's boy. Like them, I was another of his pretty acquisitions. At parties, he would smile and sigh to his cronies that the flowers and I were both beautiful to the eye. When I was being particularly backward, he would add, "And difficult to maintain."

Such pleasure he'd received from their sweet, delicate blooms. In the last years, he enjoyed nothing more in the evenings than sitting among them with me by his side or at his feet, staring at the Park below while the sun set behind us. He'd tended them himself nearly to the end, but I'd promised to maintain them after he was gone. During the last months of his life, I'd urged him to write down everything I needed to know. When afterward I'd attempted to read his notes, between the mysteries of his penmanship and the informal women's names he'd gifted individual plants, I knew less about the care of orchids than before I started.

Plus, the orchids seem to hate me. I won't say I've had any *Little Shop of Horrors* moments—though Kenneth had been an investor in the original Off-Broadway run—but the plants resist my care. None have outright expired, but not one has bloomed in the year since his death. I'll water what I think needs watering and half-heartedly mist anything that looks dry, but I can almost see the plants retreating in disappointment when I enter the room, the way old dogs lay down their heads with mournful eyes, when an imposter who's not their much-loved late master attempts to feed them.

I've tried to hire help, naturally. When I reach out to plant care firms with orchidologists and mention my address, they always reply, *The Kleinsmith Collection? Oh, no. Absolutely not.*

After the latest refusal, I had even exploded over the phone to Grosvenor & Foljambe, a private horticultural care establishment whose card one of Kenneth's oldest friends discreetly slipped me. I'd held a charity fundraiser here a month ago, and though I kept the greenhouses locked and off-limits, it was impossible to keep a certain gaggle of old gossips from peeping around the drawn blinds to spy the orchids' sorry state.

"I'm sorry," the firm's receptionist had apologized after I rang them up and dropped the old man's name. "Our manager says we just couldn't."

Hearing those words again provoked me into exploding, "Is the Kleinsmith money not good enough for you?"

There was a pause. "I'm sure your money is fine, sir," she had replied in the mildest of tones. "But the collection's reputation is so esteemed that we wouldn't dare..."

As if I'd suggested they grab some colored markers to touch up the Mona Lisa.

I am nearing the terminus to a long, sad journey. My last shot. If Luis' nephew isn't prepared to pull a miracle out of his hat, my next move will be to have Helga find someone to clear out the greenhouses for good.

I cannot help but feel guilty, though. What good is a

greenhouse without its greenery? More to the point: if I forfeit the greenhouses, why should I even continue to occupy The Campbell's famed greenhouse suite?

If professionals won't take on The Kleinsmith Collection, I sure as hell don't know how some pimply little undergrad will manage. I slide out of bed and into a short silk kimono, a souvenir of my first Tokyo Fashion Week with Kenneth. Decades have passed, so the hem lies higher than it used to, and my chest strains at the fabric. From the kitchen waft the mingled scents of ginger and vanilla, a sure sign that Helga's baking the biscuits she enjoys with her tea. They're delicious, but for the sake of my waistline, I abstain.

Out of consideration for her sensibilities, I pull on a pair of black trunks under the kimono and pad from the bedroom down the hall, where my morning pressed veggie smoothie should await.

So. This is how I envision the interview: at ten on the dot, when the little botanist shows up, I'll give him the once-over in the foyer. We will chat. If the kid seems all right, I might give him a once-over of the greenhouses. If not, out of respect for Luis, I'll at least allow him the freedom to drop my name at his next job interview. My hopes aren't high, but it's the least I can—

That's when the foyer bell jangles.

I don't get drop-ins. Visitors need to check in downstairs. They duly ring up to ask if I'm expecting callers. Only with permission would a guest receive admittance to the elevator; even then, a doorman must use a key to activate any button. How in the hell—?

The bell sounds again, shrill and clamorous. Over that, without warning, the house phone's gentler trill. I'm closer to that, so automatically I pick up the receiver. "Yes?"

For a long, loud moment, I'm suspended in time and confusion, the racket from someone leaning on my bell in one ear and Luis from downstairs babbling through the receiver in the other. I can only make out one in seven of the doorman's words. "...so sorry, Mr. Carr... he's a good boy but...on his way up...knows where I keep my elevator keys and...he's truly a good boy but..."

I've had enough. This little whippersnapper. No respect for the way things work! I don't know what that college of his teaches, but he's stumbled onto the one surefire method of flunking a job interview and making an enemy in the process. Yanking open the door, I prepare to give the lad a piece of my mind. "Now look here, kid..."

In dreamlike slow-motion, he pushes his way in. Regular time no longer applies. Seconds elongate into hours, a moment into a year. The dirty stranger from the sidewalk yesterday struts into my home as if he owns the place. With dramatic timing, the sun emerges from behind a bank of clouds; morning light seems to stream through the front windows for the sole purpose of caressing every bulge and plane of the brute's body. Could he be wearing yesterday's clothing? No, this V-neck tee is a dark gray and hugs his muscular torso even more tightly. His nipples protrude obscenely through the cotton. I recognize those jeans, though, by the ragged bottom hems, carelessly half-stuffed into a pair of beat-up red high tops.

My heart races at the sight of him, here, in my home, standing in those wretched sneakers upon my newly shampooed New Zealand wool entry hall white carpet. His hair is just as thick and full as I remembered when I had reached beneath the sheets the night before to—never mind. Down past his chin it hangs, shoved back by the wireless headphones resting on his clavicle. I stand frozen and unable to breathe, phone in one hand, as he takes a calculated look around the place.

"'Sup," he says to me with a lift of his chin. His voice is deep and resonant. "Morning, ma'am," he adds to Helga, who during the ruckus had emerged from the kitchen. She stands in the hallway, drying a glass flower vase, mouth agape, waiting to see if I need her to call someone.

Then the man runs a hand through his hair and whips it back over his forehead, still in slow motion. My breath catches in my chest at the beauty of it.

A tinny voice still emerges from the receiver in my hand. "Aw yeah, that'd be my uncle," growls the man. He reaches to divest me of the phone. "Probably fretting about his job. You're not gonna get him in any trouble, are you?" Spoken another way, the words could have come out as a threat. But from this unbearably handsome stranger, they sound more like a statement of fact.

I shake my head and allow his big, warm hands to uncurl my fingers from their grip. I almost feel disappointment when he's done, but time has regained its normal speed, and things are moving too quickly for my emotions to register. I manage to make a gesture in Helga's direction, to let her know all is well. She nods and disappears back into the kitchen.

"Yeah, everything's fine. You worry too much, old man." With a few melodic phrases in Portuguese, he shoots off a quick laugh, somehow sunnier than all the light streaming through the east-facing windows. "Yeah, yeah. I'll catch you on the way out. Later, *Tio*." He faces me, phone in one hand, staring. Moments ago, I'd been ready to lay into him. Seeing my handsome stranger from the street again, though, has made me forget what I'm doing, where I am, or how I've gotten here. "So?" He raises those thick, dark eyebrows. "You want this back?"

"Oh. Yeah. Yes." I snatch the phone and drop it upon its base. I miss, of course, and it clatters onto the glass-topped table. I ignore the damned thing. "Um. You're early."

The man stands with his hands on his hips, as if taking measure of his domain. Once more, I drink in the elaborate designs of ink etched upon his left arm.

His right wrist is also encircled by a band of dark ink. I gulp with guilt when his brown eyes bore into mine. I've been caught staring at his musculature. "Yeah. Well. I've got shit to do later. You get it. So." His narrow hips swivel to the right. "Down here, huh?"

Without permission or invitation, he's off down the hallway in the direction of the north greenhouse. "Something smells good!" he calls with a wink to Helga, breaking stride to stick his head through the kitchen archway. I try to shrug and apologize as I scamper in the man's wake. Helga's usually icily formal with strangers. She'd been Kenneth's housekeeper for forty years and was always a stickler for protocol. At this man's brusque intrusion, though, she puts a hand to her chest and...giggles. Helga. Giggling. I never thought I'd see the day.

This entire morning is getting out of hand. The nephew is already down the central hallway, poking his head through open doorways as he passes. In my kimono and bare feet, I scramble behind. Not until we both reach the leaded glass doorway does he pause; by the door rests a keypad requiring a code. By the time I catch up, he's lounging against the wall, arms crossed against his chest in a shameless show of ink and brawn, waiting. I'm a little breathless as I punch in the digits. Whether from the chase or the mere sight of him, I don't know.

"Now look here," I say, as he strides into what used to be a lush oasis and is now just twigs. That key code should have been mine to bestow, not his to demand. Yet the sight of that deep chest and that cocky, knowing smirk, those dark eyes, the expectant tilt of that sharp jawline...in the presence of all that, I'd crumbled. I had given him exactly what he wanted, without him even having to ask, and lost the opportunity to establish our footing. "You're early."

He's bent over, his index finger plunged to the second knuckle in one of the larger planters, but he turns to face me and straightens. "Yeah, you already said that."

"Look here," I say, then realize I'd already said that, too. "Our appointment was for ten and it's only..." Looking at my wrist does me no good. I have a Patek I prefer for morning wear, but I must have left the watch on the nightstand. "Too early."

"Were you asleep?"

"No, but..."

"No harm, no foul, then." With a big smile that reveals a vast expanse of pearly whiter-than-whites, the man moves a little closer. Arms once again crossed, he explains. "You see, ten doesn't work for me. I've got places to be. That's why I'm up early and getting things done instead of lounging around in a..." He waves a finger toward my outfit.

I feel judged. "Kimono."

"...nightgown," he says, at the same time.

Flames lick my cheeks. "This is a one-of-a-kind vintage *men's kimono*, hand-painted, that has been in my possession since...!"

"All right. All right." His big hands spread wide and pat the air to soothe me. There's dirt under his nails already. Hell, there's dirt permanently etching the lines of his knuckles. "Now, you gonna let me check out these orchids or what? You just stand there, look pretty, and I'll do my thing."

Everything about his behavior rubs me the wrong way. My fuse may be quite long, but I am mere inches from exploding. What's more, I am no longer Mr. Kleinsmith's 'friend,' the kept boy, the accessory that can be shoved to the side. I put in my thirty-two years. What was Kenneth's is now mine, dammit, and if this overgrown slab of Brazilian beef thinks he can push his way into my home...

Then I have another thought. This overgrown slab of Brazilian beef thinks I'm pretty? Well, *gosh*!

No. No! I have to shake my head to clear it of my

wildly careening thoughts. You've already let this get out of hand, I tell myself. Time to start over. While he moves from planter to planter, poking and prodding, I keep my voice reasonable as I follow. "I apologize for my tone. I'm cranky without my breakfast. I haven't even introduced myself. I'm John Carr-Kleinsmith, and..."

"Oh, I know who you are." The man doesn't even look up as he rounds the central bank of planters.

Once more, I feel my impatience beginning to simmer. He might as well have said he knows *what* I am, like all those friends of Kenneth's, before they fell by the wayside, who dismissed me as nothing more than a flavor of the month. "I don't know your name, though."

"My uncle didn't tell you?"

"No, he..." I'm taken slightly aback when, without warning, the man bends low over an antique, blue-glazed pot. At first, I think he's merely examining a particularly recalcitrant specimen, but with exquisite delicacy, he applies the very tip of his thick, broad tongue to a leaf. Then, smacking his lips as if tasting something acrid, he straightens up again. Would Grosvenor & Foljambe have licked the orchids quite so tenderly? "...he, uh, didn't."

His eyes boring into mine, the man advances. His biceps flex as he interlocks his fingers, then cracks them with a flurry of snaps. I am not a short man—I'm a solid five-ten—but the orchid whisperer has a couple of inches on me. The sheer bulk of him makes my heart race: those broad shoulders, the pecs that stretch his tee to the breaking point, the width and depth of him. That thick, dark hair, hanging in waves around his ears. I shiver as he approaches. "My name is Oscar," he announces in the softest and most intimate of voices.

All I can do is nod, ever so slightly. Oscar. Somehow it suits him. He smells of soap and fresh-cut grass as he closes in. I should stop staring into those deep, dark eyes, the color of smoky quartz, but I can't tear away my gaze. In my trunks, there's a stirring that I desperately hope my kimono is long enough to cover. My lips are dry; I start to moisten them, then desist, not wanting to give the impression that I'm hoping to be kissed. Oh, good lord. Is Oscar going to kiss me? Is he? He's still moving near. I am certain he's going to plant those broad lips, the color of ripe apricots, on mine.

He presses a fist against a flattened palm somehow to extract a few more knuckle pops. "I have a question for you, Johnny."

I have spent three decades under the shackles of my name's diminutive, but I don't resent hearing it from Oscar's sensuous mouth. Not at all. "What is that...Oscar?" I will say yes to anything he wants.

"What I want to know is..." For an eternity, I tremble, waiting, until in low and sultry tones, he murmurs, "Have you been fucking with the greenhouse humidity?"

"Yes," I breathe. Wait. What? From behind me, Helga's recognizable, discreet knock on the glass door brings me to my senses. "I mean, no! I haven't touched a thing," I say, pointing to a pair of touch pads on the wall as I let the housekeeper in. That saucy minx has pulled some of her own tea biscuits from the oven and popped them onto the good china for our guest. I give her the old hairy eyeball as she flutters and simpers. "The controls are there. Kenneth had them installed maybe two, three years ago. They're the same in the south greenhouse. I haven't fucked with anyone. *Anything!*" My face reddens. I've let slip more than I should.

Both Helga and I watch, rapt, as Oscar slides one of the oblong biscuits from the plate. His tongue licks out —personally, I'm thrilled at its encore appearance—and escorts half its length into his mouth. There's a crunch. His heavy jaw grinds in a circular motion as he chews. "Delicious," he pronounces, with a meaningful wink to Helga. And what does that elderly wench do? Giggles and coos like she's a teenager, instead of the staid elderly domestic I've always known. Then to me he adds, "I see your mom's got a few tricks up her sleeve. Hold up, you can't be Johnny's mom. You're way too young."

Helga is in her late seventies and looks a hundred. While she giggles and we both demur any relation, I struggle with my sudden jealousy. Why is she the one who gets his notice? Childish of me, but damn it. I saw him first! "She's the housekeeper," I finally say, adding with meaning, "and probably has things to do." Even now, as Helga reluctantly backs out through the door, I want to grind my teeth as Oscar gives her another wink and munches his biscuits with relish.

I have to get this stupid infatuation under control. Starting here, starting now. I am a fifty-four-year-old New Yorker, not a teenager. I draw myself to my full height, assume as much dignity as I can in my trunks and kimono, and clear my throat. "Now, about the orchids."

"Let me show you something," says Oscar, using the same, intimate, gravelly voice he might employ if requesting a secret liaison behind the potting bench after midnight. He's off toward the center area, where on a multi-tiered erection of Arts and Crafts blue-glazed handmade tiles sit multiple plantings. He waits until I join him to continue. "Feel how moist the soil is in this one." I obey, pressing a fingertip against the dirt. "Nah, man." He seems perplexed with me. "Get in there. Get *in* there."

I don't know what I could be doing wrong. I can feel perfectly well how crusty the top layer of dirt is, beneath my fingertips. But before I can object, he moves in close, encompasses the back of my hand with his meatier, olive-skinned paw, and digs his fat thumb into my palm. Then he extends my middle and index fingers and plunges them into the planter up to the second knuckle.

Standing close, he says, "You gotta really get *in* there,

dude." I want to melt from the warmth of him at my side, the sheer heat of his breath on my ear. "Feel how wet it is?" I do. Beneath the surface, the earth is close to sodden. But mostly I feel his hand around mine, sense his nearness. Smell his scent of a fresh field on a sunny day. "It's too much. Some of the other ones, it's too little. Most are running wild. They need pruning. These beauties aren't dead. Yet. But unless they get some tender loving care, they're gonna be. It's like, I don't know, someone's been coming in every night and slopping water from a can all over them, then calling it a day."

I clear my throat. "Wow. Shocking," I manage to gasp out. "Don't know who could've done that." It's me. It's me who does that.

"You gotta keep something about orchids in mind." Oscar still hovers over my shoulder, murmuring in my ear, manipulating my digits as he pokes them into an adjacent pot. "They're not ordinary flowers. They need extra care. Not just 'cause they're delicate. We put that added attention in because they're sexy. They're survivors. They're *dangerous*."

"Dangerous?" I want this moment to last forever, even if it is nothing more than a botany lesson with benefits.

"Oh yeah. The most dangerous flower." The hairs on my neck tremble as Oscar huffs out a laugh. "Orchids do all kinds of shady things to reproduce. Some lure bugs inside and hold them captive, while they drench them with their secretions. There's one that will trick a wasp into mating, just to cover it all over with pollen while it thinks it's getting off with another wasp. Brutal, right?" He lets out another chuckle. "All flowers are sexual organs, but orchids...they're the horniest of the bunch."

"Can you revive them?" I clear my throat and struggle to sound like a normal person, not a hypnotized dummy under a man's sexual thrall.

"We can fix things," he says, tugging my fingers from the moist soil. He places an emphasis on the word *we*.

"I pay well," I tell him.

Maybe it's the wrong thing to say, since he drops my hand like a hot potato and steps back. Immediately, I miss his proximity. "Yeah, this is the part you're not going to like."

"Money's really no objection!" I'm desperate for him to stay here and put things right. No matter how long it takes. Especially if it takes long.

"That's the thing. You rich folk." Oscar shoves his hands into his pockets and shakes his head. "Throwing money at shit is what you do, especially with problems you want to make go away. That doesn't sit right with me. I'll bill you for my expertise, sure. But if I'm investing my time here, I want what you call a reciprocal arrangement."

"Okay. Sure. Anything." I try to lean back against one of the columns supporting the half-dome and cross my legs in a casual pose, but my kimono hikes up dangerously high.

"I run a co-op garden. In the Bronx." He states the last three words like a challenge. "We plant high-yield produce for one of the local food banks. Gets the neighborhood involved."

"Oh!" I think I know where he's going with this. "I can write a check..." Wait. The exasperation in his furrowed, thick brows tells me once again I'm way off base. "You don't want a check."

"I'll take a check, all right," he laughs. "Checks are good. But, yeah...go on. You're getting there."

"You want me to...volunteer."

"There we go, Johnny-boy. That's exactly what I want."

"Well, sure," I say. "Volunteering is what I do. I'm great on a charitable board."

My reply garners from Oscar a broad, white smile. My god. How many teeth can one single man have? I would do anything to see that smile more often. "You slay me, Johnny-boy. Charitable board. Wild! I'll give my uncle the deets, and you can swing by Saturday morning, ready to go. Bright and early. Then Monday, you and I, we'll start whipping these sexy ladies into shape."

To what have I committed myself, exactly? Before I can think about it too hard, he approaches me once again with a bow-legged gait. One broad arm swings wide. Only at the last moment do I realize he wants to slap his hand into mine in a handshake, to seal the deal.

We stare into each other's eyes mutely for a moment. Suddenly—and I gasp when it happens—he drops me a wink. Then he's gone, tugging at the deep neck of his tee and striding out without a farewell.

I stagger back into a bank of pots and try to collect myself. Good god. How badly I want that man.

In the Ramble

❦

I cannot pretend that thoughts of Oscar don't dominate the rest of my day. Every waking moment, I picture those big arms, that snaking column of ink, that long, wavy hair, those white teeth. Visions of his muscles beneath a thin layer of white cotton fill my imagination through meals and a long afternoon of phone calls as I plan a fundraiser. Even that night, sitting through an interminable Bach oratorio at The Phil, I stir restlessly in my seat, waiting for the moment I can head home, crawl into bed, and reach beneath the sheets to release my pent-up frustration.

I am on fire for a man. It had been so, so long since the last time that had happened. Almost thirty years exactly, in fact.

I was twenty-four and had been living with Kenneth for two years. For a streetwise kid who'd grown up with nothing and had zero life goals, landing at The Campbell was like winning the lottery. Great food, fancy digs, no roaches in the hallways. At first, I'd taken to my new life with nothing but gratitude. I was happy to do everything Kenneth wanted of me. I let him choose my hairstyle, my clothing, my trainer. I enjoyed being his adornment. Pretty Johnny, always at his side.

Somewhere around the two-year mark, though, my

new life started to chafe. Not having a room of my own annoyed me. I was never unsupervised. Very little privacy. Could rarely jerk off. I might have been served from a silver platter, but I didn't have my own bank accounts or credit plates.

When we traveled—warm places, places with beaches, because that's what Kenneth liked—I wasn't allowed to sit when we were poolside. No, Kenneth liked me to wear nothing more than a sling slip bathing suit and stand by his lounger to show off my new muscles, so everyone would recognize what a trophy he'd acquired. At parties, I couldn't make friends or relax. I was little more than a glorified, unpaid cater waiter, passing around drinks and smiles in equal measure. Kenneth prized me like he prized his orchids: for being ornamental.

After a few months, I no longer had my own buddies. Only Kenneth's, and what a gaggle of hateful old queens they were, all his age or older. They treated me like a brainless himbo, certain I wouldn't get their quips about Sondheim, hooting with laughter when I didn't understand performance art or know who Lypsinka was. Kenneth wouldn't abide a sulk, so I'd endure their mockery, right to my face, while pretending not to understand it.

Only one of Kenneth's friends went out of his way to be kind—an older Broadway costume designer named Merle. He took me aside at a cocktail party one night, when the queens were giving me an especially tough time behind Kenneth's back. "The best thing you can do, kid," he'd whispered, "is to outlive your enemies. Cirrhosis will get most of these miserable bitches. Then you're home free."

Those words became my mantra.

And the sex—well. Kenneth was never much of a sexual creature. Sometimes he would dress me up: a harness and chaps, or cowboy boots and a ten-gallon hat, or a pair of jogging shorts, knee-high white socks, a tank top, and headband, like out of some '70s skater porn. I'd pose. He'd jerk off. At most, he expected a decorous and uncomplicated blow job, once or twice a week. I would pretend satisfaction at the end, then finish myself off in the shower while he slept, careful to keep the noise down.

I'd been promoted from scrappy pup to lap dog in no time flat. Yet that second year, the last time I would go absolutely feral, I'd had enough.

Jogging was one of the few activities I could undertake on my own, outside The Campbell, without needing to ask permission or submit to endless questioning. Kenneth approved of anything that kept me trim and fit. I loved those couple of hours in the evenings when I could don my running shoes and sweats and head out onto the streets unsupervised. I developed a route around the Central Park Lake east, past the Bethesda fountain, up to 79th, then back west.

One night in the middle of autumn, I encountered the man who became my downfall. On a bench right on the edge of the Ramble he sprawled, near a path leading toward the Tunnel, wearing jeans and a dark windbreaker. He stared at me with hunger in his eyes. I knew the look well. I used to be an occasional visitor to the Ramble before Kenneth, though mostly I'd gone to gawk. The Tunnel had been the site of many a late-night orgy, where men milled about in search of hungry holes and mouths. But of course, I dared not return, since.

The man on the bench was ugly. *Ugly*. Face like an Easter Island statue, all unmoving forehead, slitted eyes, belligerent, thick lips. Somewhere in that general area of late forties to late fifties, he hovered; creases aged his pitted skin, and bags darkened his eyes. He didn't even bother hiding his interest as I jogged by. Our eyes locked. We continued staring as I bounced past.

I don't know why—he had been truly difficult to look at, and off-putting enough to clear the floor of any gay bar—but I wanted that man more than I'd ever before wanted anyone. Maybe his unsightliness was the reason he fascinated me. Despite the face, he exuded an overwhelming, unapologetic masculinity that made me weak at the knees. He was trouble.

For the rest of my jog, I fantasized about what might have happened had I stopped in my tracks. If I'd turned around and made my way back. That run was the first time I considered cheating on the man who'd taken me in and elevated my life.

God, how badly I wanted to.

Three consecutive nights that week, I jogged the same route at the same time, hoping to encounter that ugly man sitting on that bench. Two of those nights, I'd rounded the bend with my heart pumping beyond the exercise I was giving it, wondering if he might be there. He wasn't.

On the third night, when the temperatures were starting to cool and the sun had just set, I saw him again. In that same beat-up windbreaker and jeans, he waited. An opened pack of Marlboros jutted from the pocket of his wrinkled dress shirt, and a lit cigarette hung from his thin lips. His head already turned in my direction. Like he expected me.

Oh man, that face. Just as immovable and craggy as before. Just as ugly.

Keep in mind that I was twenty-four and dumb. Yet in my head, I was convinced that it would be safer to cheat with a fellow challenged in the looks department. We were still battling a plague with no cure in those days, and my infantile logic told me that an ugly man would have fewer partners. Dumb, dumb, dumb. My dick was doing all my thinking that night. I jogged past the man, eyes locked, then stopped. I turned around to face him in the dusk.

He spread his legs wide open, settled his hand on the center seam of his denim, and squeezed. A red tip of lit tobacco danced in front of his face like a summer firefly.

Fuck. My insides churned with desire. I took a step forward. He unfolded himself from the bench, tossed the cigarette on the pavement, and stubbed it out with a twist of his foot before turning to walk away. That he wanted me to follow, he confirmed when he looked over his shoulder.

He wasn't hard to spot once he veered off the path into absolute shade dappled only occasionally by the park's streetlamps. The man was six-four, six-five, easily, and his height only added to his hulking, forbidden allure. He led me over moss-encrusted rocks and up a slope through spiky evergreen brush and low-hanging trees. Strange, how quiet it was there, though we stood in the middle of the loudest and densest city in the world. He didn't say a word. I could smell sour old tobacco on his breath as he drew close.

The man's frigid hands trespassed beneath my tee-shirt. He wrenched it and my hoodie over my head, burning my ears with their friction. The night was chilly enough that I shivered while I stood there, half-naked and waiting, but his silent admiration of my lean torso made me forget the cold. His calloused palms scraped over my still-new pecs, my flat stomach, my narrow hips. One hand snaked its way past the elastic of my sweatpants to cup my ass. When he discovered I was wearing a jock—something I'd donned earlier with him in mind—he hissed with satisfaction.

My neck craned up as I tried to kiss the compressed grimace that was his mouth, but he turned away at the last moment. Instead, he jammed my wrist through his open fly, forcing me to tug out his cock. I couldn't believe what lay within. I felt like a magician pulling knotted handkerchiefs from his top hat: more and more penis kept emerging from the denim. But this was no sleight of hand: the man packed the biggest tool I'd ever beheld. The thing had to be nine, nine and a half inches, and as thick around as a soda can. Rock hard in my hands, it must have weighed more than one of Kenneth's champagne bottles.

Good god, did I want it.

I must have betrayed my desire with a whimper, because without a word, he spun me by my hips, away from him. Anxiety rose in my throat. I knew this was my last chance to escape before I crossed this line of no return. "I can't..."

I could. The man shoved me forward, raking my naked shoulder against the closest tree. My ear scraped against the bark. Cold fingers probed my hole. Three nights in a row, I'd gone so far as to douche myself before my jog, on the off chance this very encounter might happen. Now, I started to regret it. "No, I shouldn't..."

Oh, but my body told him I should. My ass hoisted itself up at the onslaught of two of his spit-slick digits. My back arched; my feet assumed a wider stance. My mouth might be saying one thing, but he took his permission from the way I presented my hole for his invasion. I tried to protest when I heard him spit on his massive dick, but he made shushing noises. Below us, on the section of bridle path beyond that was visible through the thick branches, a cruiser strolled by, whistling, unaware of how close we were.

Beads of perspiration broke out on my forehead as I felt that monster log nudge at my hole. I hadn't been fucked in—well, it wasn't something Kenneth enjoyed, much as I wanted it. I'd tried to train myself out of desiring dick in my ass. I'd told myself there was more to sex and a relationship than having my guts rearranged. So, I was both out of practice and fearful of what a tool that size might do to me. "Please don't..."

He did. The first thrust seared like a hot knife through flesh. My cry of mingled anguish and relief cut through the night, equally sharp, only to be silenced by his tobacco-scented hand clamped over my mouth. "Shut the fuck up, boy," he snarled in my ear as he pushed deeper. The stranger's voice was little more than a rumble of bass in his chest.

Again, though my mind told me I'd gone too far, my body betrayed me. My hips shoved back, welcoming him deep into my guts. Surely, this was what I had been made for: giving up my hole to a stranger in the park, while stragglers below wended their ways among the Ramble's shadows.

His insistent battering against that sweet spot deep inside unloosened my inhibitions. By the time he worked those final three inches inside, already I was making justifications for what I was doing. I wasn't getting it from home, so why not here and now? This man was a one-time slip that I would never make again. Yeah, I was taking a health risk by letting him inside me raw, but I could cajole him to pull out before he filled me with his ejaculate. Fuck. *Ejaculate* was a Kenneth noun. This man was going to fill me with his spunk. His jizz. His baby batter.

I don't know how long we went at it like that, copulating athletically in that forgotten and overgrown nook hidden from sight. At one point, I began hanging onto the tree trunk in front of me for dear life, because dear God, did that man love to fuck. Maybe he couldn't often find holes able to accommodate his length and girth. Now he had one, he had no intention of letting it escape. I knew he wouldn't pull out when he shot. Maybe I counted upon it.

No, I needed degradation from the ugly stranger. The fact that he was so unpleasant-looking somehow made our coupling hotter. Cheating with a hottie would have been boring. Giving it up to someone repellent was unexpected. Twisted. My reward was this massive baseball bat of a member that plugged relentlessly away

point, desperate, I walked nine blocks down Broadway to the building where I knew Kenneth's friend Merle lived. Though I looked like a transient, the doorman there allowed me to speak to him on the desk phone.

"Johnny, Kenneth will not appreciate it if I let you stay here," he'd told me on the line. I could hear genuine regret in his voice. He had a soft spot for me, like he might for a friend's puppy he didn't have to walk or clean up after.

I'd begged. I'd pleaded. But Merle didn't budge. I could not blame him. Kenneth was good to friends but turned his back on those who disappointed him. Like I had that night. "Can you tell him...how miserable I am?" I begged, vainly trying to keep my voice down so the doorman wouldn't overhear. "That I'm sorry. That I won't do it again."

"I'll try. Johnny...wait outside a minute," he said, before disconnecting.

A few minutes later, Merle's doorman brought out an oversized puffy coat to wear. I think it had belonged to Merle's late mother. But it was a damned sight warmer than what I had on.

I was sitting outside The Campbell on the curb at seven-thirty the next morning, shivering despite the gifted coat, when Kenneth joined me. I don't know whether he'd ventured out on his own, or if at shift change the daytime doorman had notified him I loitered out there.

He didn't give a damn that he was wearing his silk pajamas, bathrobe, and slippers out onto the street. He was still more elegantly dressed than anyone else on Central Park West. Not seeming to care what an odd pair we made, he sat down beside me on the concrete. I said nothing.

"So. Did you get it out of your system?" he asked, not unkindly, as he gazed toward the park.

I nodded. My cracked, parted lips to say, "Yes, sir."

"That's that, then." He patted my knee, then used it to stand up. "Let's get you inside."

I accepted his extended hand with gratitude.

See, I was nearly feral, once. Until the real world scared it out of me, I'd thought that wildness was gone for good. Now that I am on my own, it's come roaring back.

Spud Man

❧

When the town car abandons me at Cultivate Co-Op Garden early Saturday morning, I'm a little taken aback. Not by the tall fences topped with razor wire. Those adorn the whole city. Not by the grime or the worn, weathered concrete running as far as the eye can see. No, what astonishes me is how damned wholesome the enterprise is: an entire city block, sliced at a diagonal at one corner, that's a model of order and greenery. As if an oasis has bloomed in a forgotten corner of the Bronx, shadowed by two major artery overpasses on one side and a railway bridge on the other, and nobody noticed.

Although it is only seven in the morning and the ground lies raw and wet from the night's rain, already a dozen folk bustle around the enclosure. They push wheelbarrows and transport baskets of pots from one area to another, chattering happily. Someone lays a hose between neat rows of raised earth. Other men and women kneel in the dirt, tending to what has already been planted. It's quite an organization.

I'd been tipped off by Luis, the previous evening, that his nephew expected me this morning to—get this —garden. Dumb of me, but I honestly didn't realize. Big names and corporate honchos are the mainstays of nonprofit boards. Because of their hectic calendars,

135

governing committees sometimes meet in weird corners of the day. I thought I had been recruited to raise funds, not raise veggies.

At least Luis gave me enough of a heads-up to create a look suitable for...well, I don't really know how gardens work. If I did, I wouldn't be in this mess. Lugging around a watering can has been the extent of my commitment. Look how that's turned out.

As I wave off the car and approach the open gates in the block's center, I wonder why I'm here. A corrugated tin shed sits next to the entrance, its inner walls hung with notices and clipboards. A tiny person with short, dark hair and judging eyes steps out the moment I draw close. "Good morning," I say, looking up and down the rotund, overalled figure with as much interest as they seemed to have for me. "I'm here because..."

"*Oscaaaaaar!*" blares the short-haired young person, deep from the diaphragm. "Boss! You're gonna want to see this!" We contemplate each other while we wait. "Manuel. They/them pronouns," they say at last, with a scornful look at my outfit.

"Johnny!" Oscar leaps through the mud, yelling my name so loudly that it saves the trouble of having to introduce myself to anyone. Time once again slows. All the new sights, all the noise from the overpasses and the river—everything fades away as I gawk at the object of my infatuation bounding through the mud. A fitted baseball cap turned backward tamps down his wavy mane; an apron of sorts covers his pullover hoodie and utility pants from chest to knee. He stuffs a grimy pair of gardening gloves in his back pocket. "You made it. You, uh, ready for work?"

His thorough survey of my outfit inclines me to believe I've severely misjudged what folks wear to garden. Manuel still goggles as if seeing an alien. Volunteers nearby have stopped what they're doing to lean upon their rakes and hoes and stare. Not that I'd recognize a hoe to save my life.

As if giving voice to what everyone's thinking, Oscar clears his throat and asks, "Hey now...what're you wearing there, buddy?"

What I'm wearing is a look that's pretty dressed-down for me: a pair of Ralph Lauren jeans so casual I hadn't even had them tailored, though of course they were pressed. I had paired them with one of Ralph's signature sweaters featuring a 13-starred American flag woven on the front. Maybe it's the Louis Vuitton denim jacket they're having problems with? They're gawking like they've never seen a Damier Graphite pattern before.

"Dude, did you wear suede boots to a garden?" blurts Manuel.

"Why, yes, they're..." I snap my mouth shut. My defenses go up whenever I suspect I'm being mocked. Though Manuel is just plain horrified by what's on my feet, everyone else in the vicinity is barely suppressing sniggers. I search for signs of ridicule in Oscar's face. Swear to God, if this man has set me up to be scorned, the Damier Graphite and I will stalk across the street and text for the car in the biggest direct cut any of these folk have ever seen.

Yet Oscar only seems deeply concerned. "I was gonna have you get your hands dirty getting some seedlings in, but Johnny, in that getup...and those shoes..." Having seen how the Cultivate Co-Op Garden's muddy grounds, I too have qualms about the morning's sartorial choices. "Manuel. Let's get him an apron."

"If you say so, boss." From within the corrugated shack, Manuel unhooks a smock that is, if it's possible, even dirtier than the mud. I try to wave it off, but they're determined, and pretty soon Ralph Lauren is getting cozy with something that ought to be incinerated. "There's always potato duty," Manuel says to Oscar, as they cinch me from behind, a little too tightly.

"I'm thinking the same thing. All right, big boy.

You'll be prepping potato seed pieces in the tent." He nods toward a large enclosure at the garden's far end. The structure is roughly the same size and half-dome shape as one of my own greenhouses, but instead of glass and metal, it's constructed of aluminum piping and white vinyl sheeting. "And I'm the man who's gonna get you there. You ready?" He takes a wide stance with his work boots and hunkers down.

"No." I blink as he stretches out his arms and shakes them a little before forming them into a wide cradle. Surely, he wouldn't attempt to lift me. "Absolutely not," I say, as he nears. "Nope. No!"

"Oh, it's gonna happen." He lunges. The object of my infatuation catches me from the side, scoops me into the air, and hoists me into his arms. Instinctively, my hands clutch for a hold around his neck. I am old enough to remember Richard Gere sweeping Debra Winger off her feet at the end of *An Officer and a Gentleman*, and while the co-op gardeners aren't exactly cheering like in that film, they whoop and catcall enough to make me blush. Through the mud he trudges, squelching with every step. I'm too flustered and embarrassed to enjoy the moment, but I admit to butterflies in my stomach when Oscar turns to me with a smile and says, in the most intimate of tones, "Gotta keep the kicks tidy. Right?"

I'm gasping too dramatically to reply. I should be relishing every moment of this plodding, intimate journey. The smell of him, green and earthy above the scents of mud and recent rainfall. The warmth of his ink-covered arms around my backside, embracing me. His sidelong glances, gauging my reaction to his manhandling. Like an idiot, I fret about whether I'm too heavy for him. I know holding my breath is ridiculous and that it makes no difference to my weight, but I inhale anyway.

The garden folk have pitched their tent around a foundation of pallets to support the tables and storage within. Oscar finally deposits me on the wood. "That was entirely unnecessary," I wheeze. "I could've gone barefoot."

"Nah." He bestows another of his flirty winks. Its sudden appearance makes me want to giggle and coo like Helga, but I manage a straight face. "It was my pleasure. You'll be cozy in here by yourself. I'll get someone to show you the ropes."

I try to hide my considerable disappointment at being abandoned. "Okay. See you later, I guess."

He pauses at the tent's flap, turns, and grins. "Oh, I'll check in. Gotta keep an eye on my special volunteer."

Despite the shivers running up and down my spine, I manage a casual nod. "Okay, bro." Internally, I wince. Bro? Where the hell did that come from?

Preparing the potatoes for planting turns out to be easy enough. Someone had piled an enormous quantity of knobby tubers on a long table. A kindly senior woman with graying hair and an accent reminiscent of some spice-scented island arrives in the tent to show me how to take one, check the surface for eyes and their small sprouts, and divide it into small sections, each chunk with two or preferably three eyes. These I set aside on a ventilated tray to be dried and treated before planting, later in the week.

The task is one I can carry out sitting on a stool without ruining my expensive clothing, and uncomplicated enough that it doesn't require my entire attention. My instructor drives home that it's a simple chore for a simple person when she comments that usually they save potato prep for kids to do, but Mr. Jenkins hadn't brought his twin grandchildren that morning. Great.

No matter. Okay, so I wasn't out there beyond the flap that waved back and forth in the morning wind, hefting up heavy bags of fertilizer with big, confident arms like Oscar. I wasn't tossing reclaimed concrete into wheelbarrows and anchoring the chunks into the dirt to mark discrete plots or kneeling down in the muck to weed. No one could say I wasn't doing my part. Maybe in the distant future (how long did it take for them to grow? Months? A couple of years?) someone might choose a sack of food bank potatoes that had sprung from my tidy, three-eyed chunks.

I like that idea. It keeps me motivated for the first couple of hours.

Chopping potatoes is solitary work, though, and no one really remembers I'm there. Maybe it's safer to keep me out of the way, the know-nothing privileged white guy who's a pebble between the cogs of their well-oiled machine. Sure, give that guy the work usually saved for kids with the attention span of a gnat. Stow him out of sight and out of mind. I'll probably step out later and find everyone gone and the gates locked. Scaling the fence will ruin my Louis Vuitton denim. Wouldn't that just be the way things go? How long have I been here, anyway? Is it night yet?

"Hey." The plastic flaps part with a rustle. Oscar steps inside, covered in grime. Somehow, it suits him. "Most everybody's taking a lunch break. Don't know if you brought anything, but…" He hoists a brown paper sack in one hand and a plaid plastic thermos in the other. "I can share."

Feebly, I protest that I'm fine. To be honest, I'd assumed that if we needed lunch, we'd send out for food.

Ignoring me, he withdraws two apples from the sack, keeps one for himself, and plants the other on the table. "My gift to you. Potatoes look great. Nice of you to be our spud man for the day."

"Thanks. Hope I can live up to the mighty legacy of the Jenkins twins." I heft up the apple and rub it against my sweater to give it a shine. "How old are they, anyway? Six, seven?"

"Ten."

"Fantastic. Hope I've given everyone a good laugh." The words sound more bitter than I intend.

Oscar removes his cap to reveal a crown of tamped-down, shiny hair. He shakes out his mane like a dog after its bath, then sits at the table beside me. "Come on, dude. I couldn't have you doing dirty work. Not in that getup." I sigh as he unscrews the cap of his thermos. "Besides, no one's laughing at you. I mean. A little, maybe."

"Mmmm. Fuck 'em." Holding an actual conversation with the man feels good. Natural. "An old friend once told me that the best thing I could do is to outlive my enemies."

There's a wily look in Oscar's eye as he meets my gaze. "Does that make me the enemy?"

I study him boldly as I crunch into the apple. When I'm finished chewing, I say, "You trying to be?" When he laughs, I join in. From the thermos's mouth, he pours a thick red substance that's still warm enough to produce some steam. I recognize the sweet smell of tomato sauce immediately. "Are you actually eating Spaghettios?"

"With meatballs, yeah. Want some?"

"No, thank you." I decline to point out that I've outgrown pasta from a can and instead watch him slurp a mouthful straight from the thermos cup. "Back in Nebraska, when I was a kid, and if my dad could be bothered, the old slob used to open a can of that mess and plop it in a bowl. Not warmed up or anything."

"Seriously?" Oscar tilts back his head to let the oleaginous mess slip down his throat, then pours himself another helping. "Bumpy childhood, huh?"

"Something like that." I am not fond of revisiting my earlier years.

"Then you moved to the city. Found your man." He swallows another huge mouthful of soggy noodles. "How old were you then?"

I clear my throat, wary. "Twenty-two."

"A *baby*. And him?"

"Fifty-one. Look..."

He cuts off anything defensive I might say with a simple question, one that no one had ever asked me before. "Did you love him?"

"I mean..." I struggle to find a way to answer truthfully without sounding entirely heartless. "He was never a warm and fuzzy type, but yeah, we had a good relationship. I was there for him until the end. I was fond of him."

I've left myself open for the undeniable observation: *and fond of his money*. Sure. I was grateful to be secure and taken care of for the first time in my life. I'd traded away my youth for Kenneth's protection; I'd swallowed my pride as easily as Oscar gulped down canned pasta. My life was a devil's bargain. Until recently, I thought I was at peace with the deal.

But Oscar doesn't point out any of these things. "Did he, you know?" He waggles his thick eyebrows in comic exaggeration. "Keep you happy?" When I erupt with a shocked laugh, he adds, "Come on, he was an old man. Could he keep up?"

"I'm older now than he was when we met!"

"Sorry, but you don't have an old vibe." A jolt of electricity runs from my leg to my spine: Oscar has placed his hand on my knee. "Anyone can tell you've got lots of juice in you."

"I...um, thanks."

"Come on." From the adjacent stool, he leans forward and plants the other hand on my opposite thigh. I feel a stirring deep inside as he looms close. "Don't you think so? I think there's a rascal inside itching to get out. Isn't there?"

How does he know so much about me? Gossip, of course. I am used to decades of tittle-tattle behind my back. A generation of doormen and hired help and maintenance whispering about what I might have done to get where I am. No doubt this man has talked about me with his uncle.

In the back of my mind, though, I worry. From Oscar himself, I had learned that something beautiful, something sexy, could be dangerous. Some orchids trap insects for their own agenda. What if Oscar is using something he learned to manipulate me?

On the other hand, do I really mind being manipulated if it means his hands all over me?

I'm hyper-aware of Oscar's physicality. He's so close. Even through layers of apron and hoodie, his body heat blasts like the open door of a furnace. With almost no distance between us, it would be nothing to reach out and rub that sharp jawline, covered in scruff. I could run my fingers through this young man's hair or pull his face to mine. He stares into my eyes, palms pressing into my knees, waiting for my answer. I, however, am too frozen to respond.

He takes the initiative. From my clutch, he removes the apple and lets it bounce onto the table. Without a word, he wraps his enormous hand around mine and guides it between his spread legs, so slowly I can count dozens of my thudding heartbeats. I lose sight of it as he shepherds my wrist beneath his apron and between his open thighs. This isn't happening, surely. I make a pretense of pulling back, but now that he has me, he's not letting go.

"That's right," he whispers, nodding with encouragement. "It's okay. I think you want it." Oscar is correct. I've never wanted anything more. But I have lived too long in my diminished self to let go in this moment. "Touch it."

My lips part in an involuntary sigh. My cupped hand collides with his basket, as we used to call it in my day. Through a heavy shield of thick cotton, I can feel the heft of his balls, the fire emanating from his crotch. My thumb runs up and down the length of his meaty protrusion. He's not even fully hard; beneath my hand, I can feel his cock shift and lengthen. The man is huge.

"You like that?" he whispers, his mouth scant inches from mine.

"I..." Behind me, I hear the sound of vinyl sheeting rustling, then a hasty murmured apology. Oscar's eyes flick to the side, looking beyond. Though he doesn't release my hand, he sits up a little straighter. Someone has peeked into the tent.

All those memories from that bad night long ago flood back. Sitting on the cold curb, having no one on my side, not knowing if I would have a place to sleep. I'd risked everything on one unwise decision and nearly paid the price.

I am a man of means, yet fear is still making my decisions. "I need to go," I mutter, retrieving my hand from its warm cocoon. "I've got...things."

"Johnny." Oscar's voice is hoarse. "Don't."

"Yeah, I've got appointments all afternoon. Hey, um. Thanks for..." Never mind. In that moment, I give up. I am done. Done with gardening, done with Oscar. Done with having my hopes raised and my emotions played with. I give that dangerous young man a nod without any eye contact and stumble from the tent, untying my smock in a hurry.

Shoes be damned. I know they're a lost cause the moment they squelch in the muck. But I trudge on, slopping through mud and puddles to make my escape. "Johnny!" I hear from behind me, but I don't turn to see if Oscar follows.

"Don't..." Manuel has emerged from the shed to gesticulate wildly. When I look down, I'm inches away from treading on a row of sprouts. "Watch out for the...!" On my other side are sticks and vines inside of wire cages. I hadn't seen any of it. Obviously, I'm not cut out to be a gardener.

"Damn it," I say. I make an athletic leap to a pile of concrete chunks that have seen the jackhammer, and then to a drier patch of land near the fence, nearly twisting my ankle in the process. It's not the exit I'd intended to make, let's just say.

Manuel leaps back as I nod and stagger out the gate. "Here," I say, intending to toss them the gardening apron in a huff. But because of what kind of person I am, I pause and neatly fold the damned thing, then pass it over with a thank-you before sprinting away, huff-free. I don't look behind. Lot's wife did that at Sodom, and look where it got her.

I had wanted to follow where Oscar led. What I desired had been in my literal grasp. But when push came to shove, I couldn't unclench. That side of myself disappeared years ago.

Maybe it's too late to change.

Late Night Meeting

❦

When the house phone rings Tuesday night after I've slipped into bed, I'm annoyed: the closest extension is a good thirty feet away. Kenneth refused to allow any technology more than a sad old electric alarm clock in our bedroom. That will need to change. Kenneth doesn't live here anymore.

The electronic trill continues as I slide into some slippers and a robe. I pad out into the hallway outside the bedroom to see what downstairs wants. "Yes?"

I recognize Luis's voice immediately. "Sorry to bother you so late, Mister Carr, but um, there's a delivery..."

"I'll pick it up in the morning, Luis." Was this worth rousing me from bed?

"Ah." There's sputtering at the line's other end. I get the distinct impression he might be covering the receiver to hold another conversation. He's back. "It needs a signature, urgently. Can I bring it to you?"

"Why not?" I sigh and hang up. No need to dash for clothing. I already wear a tank and boxers to sleep in, and my robe hangs from my shoulders, so I won't be shocking the downstairs staff with my naughty bits. I stumble down the hallway and through the living area.

By the time I unlock the foyer door, the elevator

already sounds its soft chime. "Listen," I say, as the door slides back, then stop talking.

Oscar plants a Timberland boot onto the Italian mosaic. He wears a pair of dark gray sweats, the white tie in a neat bow at his waist. A dark blue flannel shirt, its sleeves rolled up above his elbows, hangs open; beneath it, a white V-neck. He clutches a folder beneath his arm. His head hangs low, almost sheepish.

His rotund little uncle steps out from behind. "My nephew is very persuasive..." he starts explaining.

"You've been avoiding me, Johnny," rumbles Oscar. Is he actually hurt? Hard as I try, I cannot conceive of someone with his looks and in the prime of his life suffering from wounded pride.

"Mister Carr, if I've overstepped..."

It's not the first time Luis has overstepped, but for the sake of keeping the peace, I wave him down. I'm going to take this one on the chin. "I'll talk to him."

"You will?" The doorman looks from his nephew to me and back again, obviously anticipating trouble. "When he insisted on seeing you this late, I said..."

"I'll be fine. You can get back downstairs."

"All right, Mister Carr." I've never seen anyone look so dubious, but Luis backs into the elevator and punches the lobby button. "Don't cause any trouble, now." I nearly reply that I won't, until I realize he's talking to his nephew.

The moment the doors slide closed, Oscar demands, "Why are you ignoring me?"

"I haven't been." I'm lying. From his uncle, Oscar had extracted the number for the landline Kenneth insisted on keeping. He'd called Saturday afternoon and had quite the chat with Helga about whether I'd gotten home intact and to apologize for the state of my clothing. Yesterday, the day we'd agreed he'd thoroughly assess both greenhouses, I'd cut and run to arrange a first lunch date suggested by a matchmaking service—a guy who was perfect on paper, but so tedious over our sushi that I'd considered giving up dating altogether. "Okay. I have."

Luis is long gone. Just the two of us stand in the foyer. Even though we talk in low tones, our voices still reverberate in the small space. "I wasn't lying about a delivery." He pats the folder and hands it over. "Didn't know if you were a digital or analog kind of guy, so I covered the bases. Did an inventory of both greenhouses. Your husband kept his plantings in zones, so the care's a little different in each. It's all in here." He thrusts his tattooed arm in his sweats, searching for something. "Also in a spreadsheet, on here." He passes me a little flash drive embedded in a comical plastic robot.

I turn it over in my hand, thinking it both highly unprofessional and disarmingly endearing.

"Two more things and I'll go." From his shirt pocket, he draws two small digital devices on metal spikes. "The green one measures moisture. The yellow one, pH. I've put the levels you want for each zone in the report. You've already got the right stuff in the greenhouses. It'll take some practice to get the balance right, but you're a smart guy. I've got faith in you. The pollinating, though, might take..."

I stare at him, astonished. Abandoning me? Already? "So that's it?"

"That's it." He drops the formality and lets his exasperation show. "Come on. Don't give me those big puppy dog eyes. When you ghosted me, I got the message. You want me out of your hair."

"I did," I babble in a panic. "But I don't."

"Look, dude." His head still hangs low; his long locks nearly cover his face. "I misjudged the other day. I saw the way you would look at me. A blind man could see the way you look at me. I thought you wanted... well, I was wrong. Usually, my radar is better than that." When I don't reply, he raises his hands and backs off. "Okay then. Be seeing you."

"Wait." I'd been a fool for letting an opportunity with him slip from my fingers. "Don't go."

He hesitates. "No?"

"No." Foolish as I feel, an old geezer in his night-wear and slippers standing before a young buck, I know this is my last chance. How many last chances really are left for me at this stage in my life? I clutch his offerings to my chest for protection. "I'm sorry. I'm an idiot. You didn't misjudge. I was looking. Christ, all I want to do is look at you. In the garden, when we were alone, I got scared. I haven't...it's been so long."

Oscar raises a hand to his chin. With thought, he strokes his beard. "You've got everything anybody could ever want. And you're scared?"

"I am a tired old man. You're a beautiful young one."

He dismisses my objections with a laugh. "You're not old."

"You know that I'm older than my husband when he met me—and he was an old man."

"I told you, shit's different these days." He plunges his hands deep into the pockets of his sweats. "Guys now don't get old until later. A man like you is a hot daddy." Oscar closes the space between us. His big eyes stare into mine, unblinking. "I like daddies."

I tremble as he nears. "Really."

"I worried you thought I was on the make. Like, I wanted to be your sugar baby. Or that I was just trying to sweeten you up for the sake of the co-op garden." On a dime, his voice switches from soft and hopeful to frank. "I mean, you already committed to a donation. Before I tried to...you know."

"Yeah. I did."

"I'm not after your dough, Johnny. I'm always going to be a Spaghettios guy. Your pasta comes in fancy shapes."

"It's still noodles." Time to shoot my shot. I clear my throat and step back. "You coming inside?"

"Yeah. I'm coming inside." The gleam in his eye makes me shiver.

From the foyer through the living area and down the hallway to the master suite is a long trek. I can't help but look over my shoulder every few steps to make certain he follows. Whenever I catch his eye, he's looking not at the artwork, not at the tiny lit inset alcoves with Kenneth's treasures, not inside my exercise room, but at me. Only at me. And he smiles, which already makes my risk worthwhile.

My bed is just as I left it: picture perfect on one side, linens rumpled and folded back on the other. The bed of someone who used to share with another but now sleeps alone. I turn, hiding my expectant panting with a deep breath.

"What do you want?" Oscar rises from removing his boots, just outside the door. He steps forward, expectation on his face.

A question with too many answers. But as he draws close and I feel his warm, calloused hands wrap around my forearms, I'm emboldened to be honest. "I want you inside me."

"Where?" The word's hardly more than an exhalation; I can feel the syllable waft upon his breath to my lips. "Where do you want me?"

I think of that forbidden moment in the gardens. "I want you in my hand."

At my soft response, he closes his grip around my right wrist to guide me to my goal, just as he had the other day. This time, however, he insinuates it downward, behind his elastic waistband. My fingers dive into his sweatpants, seared by the heat within. This time, I don't shy away. I find my prize through a layer of white cotton. In my palm, it thickens and throbs. I can't believe how fat and weighty he is.

"I want it in my mouth."

This time, Oscar reaches out and pulls my face to his, gently pressing his lips to mine. He tastes of distant spearmint. We share the most tentative of kisses; afterward, he pauses, gauging my response. "You like that?"

"Yes, I do."

He grins. "Those the only places you want my hog?"

I shake my head. "In me." The admission—a simple two words—makes my legs weaken. I cannot believe I say them aloud. "I want your cock in my hole." He nods, approving.

Without being told, I slip my hand into his briefs. My fingers massage the serpent stirring within. From base to tip, I explore, while in my mind, I try to envision the monumental object in my grasp. Thick all the way through, but even more massive at the base. A forest of pubes. Uncut, which thrills me after more than half a lifetime of seeing only my late husband's pale, polite, circumcised pecker.

"Oh fuck," I growl in so feral a tone that I don't even recognize my own voice. "I need this big dick deep in my butt. Please."

"Yeah," he whispers, rasping his words. "I'm gonna get in that pussy. Don't you worry."

His language makes me shiver violently, almost as if I'm orgasming. No one has ever called my hole that before. His casual use of the word feels transgressive. Wrong. Bad.

And I am excited by a bad boy.

"Just one question," he says, rubbing his hips against mine. I nod, allowing it. "Your mom's out, right? Because when I get in that sweet hole, I'm gonna be making some noise."

"My m...?" A moment passes before I can clear the fog from my lust-addled brain. "Helga's not my mom, she's..." Only at the last moment do I catch the mischievous glint in his eye. The fucker is messing with me. "Helga has her own apartment. Probably her own high-rise, with what Kenneth was paying her. No one will hear."

"Don't be too sure." Tugging my hand out of his

pants, he shoves me onto the mattress. "You haven't heard me holler."

As if compensating for the times I watched him from afar in seeming slow motion, now that he's astride me, everything moves too quickly. His rough hands push and paw at my torso, yanking my tank top below my pits. I feel his lips on a pec, then his teeth tugging at my tender nipple. The jolt of his grazing forces me to inhale sharply; he draws an encore performance by moving to the other side. Somehow, he's managed to yank down my boxers into a tangle around my knees. My dick strains into the air, yearning. Oscar stands and wrenches off his flannel and tee, then flings them across the bedroom, while I struggle out of my robe.

My tiny nightstand lamp throws a feeble light that catches Oscar's dick sidelong, casting an ominous shadow that looms toward the hall. I'd held it in my hand only moments before, but even my imagination hadn't prepared me for the sight of this beast. Thick veins spiderweb the nut-brown surface; a bulbous purple head forces wide the foreskin's opening. Oscar's dick looks angry. I've awoken the animal without fully considering that I'm its prey.

"You like, daddy?" He's eyeing me. Relishing my shock and awe.

I'd spent a lifetime as one man's boy. This sudden promotion takes me aback. His unexpected gusto in calling me *daddy*, though, prompts me to stiffen further. "I'm proud of how beautiful my boy is," I whisper, barely able to form the words. He nods, pleased, and turns to the side, showing me his meat in profile. How can it stay so unrelentingly rigid for so long? Rock hard, it points at the windows overlooking the Park. "Fuck," I whisper, as I kick off my boxers.

My own dick is average. Nothing to be ashamed of, yet nothing that would turn heads. When Oscar approaches and shoves me backward into the pillows, then kneels between my spread legs to press his massive wiener atop mine, he makes me look and feel like a mere boy. His is so dark, so thick, so covered with thick pubes and imposing in shape in size. Mine is pale and hairless in comparison. The contrast causes me to gasp. I follow it up with a moan, as he presses his impossibly furry chest against my smooth skin and wraps me in his embrace.

"Such a hot daddy," he whispers in my ear. I laugh, helpless, as his lips scrape across my ear and down my jaw. They tease my neck, nibble again at my nipple. He hoists my left arm high above my head and dives into it with his face, huffing from my armpit. "You smell so good," he says, inhaling deeply, the same way some men might hit a bottle of poppers. "Like cinnamon. Spice."

"And everything nice?" I automatically finish, laughing some more. He's moved on to the other armpit now, wiping his face against it as if trying to cover himself with my scent.

Oscar doesn't get the reference, I guess. "I'm sure gonna be nice to you tonight," he promises. He finishes off with a deep huff, then climbs atop me. "If that's what you want."

His fingers entwine with mine as he pushes the backs of my hands into the mattress. I shiver as I make a realization. "You might be the first man to ask what I want."

I think I spy pity in his eyes at my words, but he quickly composes himself. Tendrils of his hair tickle my face as he leans down. "So, tell me."

"I want..." I struggle to choke down my guilt at saying the words aloud. "I want to be used. I want to be..." He nods, encouraging. "I want to be a cocksucker. Your cocksucker."

"You want me to use you, huh?" I don't have to answer aloud. At his question, my excited cock leaps up to slap him in the abdomen. "You need me to be selfish."

"Yes." The syllable arrives as a sharp hiss that cuts

through the stillness of the sterile bedroom. "Use me. Fucking use me."

Oscar's lips curve in the barest hint of a smile. His eyes glimmer. I sense his already impossibly hard cock stiffen against the curve of my hip. "Oh, I'm gonna use you, Dad," he promises as he grinds against me. "No doubt about that."

"Please."

"You might regret asking. It might get rough. I might call you names."

"*Please*. Call me anything."

"I might make both your holes mine." That gleam in his eyes intensifies. "If I do, you know I'll stretch them wide open." I know exactly what he's doing, and my heart flutters because of it: he's taking time to confirm that his intentions align with my needs. He's reading me like a book and laying out a plan for my approval. It's a smooth, less awkward version of what the kids these days call consent, and it makes me even hotter for him. "This big cock will make you gape, daddy."

Our encounter isn't one-sided, though. He's also telling me his own desires. Awkward as it feels to highlight the gap in our ages, I reciprocate with, "That's what I need, son."

Immediately, I can tell I've said the right thing. He grinds his hips against mine with increased intensity. "Gonna take it out on my dad."

"Do it," I beg. "Dad needs his boy."

I must be doing the dad thing right, because Oscar growls and presses his lips against mine. His tongue invades deep into the recesses of my mouth. I throw my arms around his broad back, relishing every abrasion his chest fur leaves upon my skin. My mind is too overwhelmed to process how I'm enjoying a passionate embrace with the stranger I'd first admired less than a week ago. Instead, I shut it off and drift upon a cloud of sensations: the almost painful crush of his mouth, his beard's coarseness. How he stabs at me with his blunt club as if trying to fashion a new hole. The heat of his breath in my ear, the sensation of his rugged fingers as they twist my nipples.

I'm being grabbed by the shoulders and hauled onto the nest of pillows he builds against the headboard. There he lays me flat upon my back, head propped upright. The bed bounces as he removes the rest of his clothing, save for a pair of black athletic socks. Never has this bedroom been so messy. Never has it seen such sexual energy. Thirty years I've slept and woken in this room, but tonight is the first time I've come alive within its four walls.

At my feet, he kneels, towering above. I watch with anticipation as his lips exude a quantity of spit; gravity draws it down into a long strand that breaks only when it reaches his navel. The wetness splats onto his cock. He uses his right hand to spread the stuff across its skin, making it glisten in the room's dim light. "That ass of yours is mine, Old Man."

Is it a threat? A promise? I hope both. His palm and fingers can barely encompass that thick, lustrous hog. His knees shuffle forward, spreading wide to straddle my ankles, my knees, my hips. Closer and closer, his weapon advances.

"That's right." His voice has hardened into a snarl. "Might be the last time you see it for a while. Your boy's gonna have it stuffed in a hole, here on out."

I spare a glance for his face. His brows furrow; his lips press in a smirk. His beauty leaves me breathless. "Make me yours."

"Suck it," he demands, as that brown, veiny monster nears.

I have no choice but to obey. My mouth opens, but the actual onslaught of so much hard meat forcing it wide causes my jaw to ache. Such sweet pain, though! My eyes stream as the head hammers against my throat, demanding that it stretch. I'm unsure if I can cooperate.

Yet he gives me no choice.

Hot tears stream down both sides of my nose as I look upward. He flexes his biceps, showing off like the cocky bastard he is. Impaled by his cock with nowhere to escape, even if I wanted to, all I can do is inhale through my nostrils and blink away the water blurring my vision. I've no choice but to endure his face-fucking.

Endure. Hell. I relish it. I have craved this abuse since that night in the Ramble with the ugly man who recognized me as a cheap cocksucker and used me without a second thought. This is what I've longed to be: just a mouth. A mere hole for superior tools. A warm, moist place for plundering. As if reading my mind, Oscar stares down at me and whispers, "That's right...cocksucker."

Cocksucker. The word works magic on me. Three syllables that free me from privilege and responsibility, from the layers of designer clothing and fashionable accessories with which I've armored myself through the years. *Cocksucker.* That's exactly what I am. Nothing more. I'm meant to be on my knees with a man's prize buried deep in my gullet. I was born to give pleasure to men like Oscar.

Cocksucker. His use of that disparagement liberates what few impediments remain. My jaw comes un-hinged; my trachea maximizes its aperture. His last couple of inches nestle deep, as if my throat was custom made for him.

"Fuck yeah," I hear him moan. His eyes are closed, now. His head falls back, sending hair cascading over his shoulders. "Feels good, daddy. *Fuck*, you do it right."

That's my purpose. Making men feel good. The only reply I can offer, however, is a choke and a gargle.

"Hang on, baby," he says. I feel his big hands cradle my skull, his fingers wrapping around it like a basketball ready for dunking. Instead, though, he pulls his cock out all the way and shoves it back in, once more testing and teasing the back of my throat. I shudder, then refuse to give in to my gag reflex. Everything in this moment should be about this cock. Forget my discomfort, fuck my misgivings. Pay attention to nothing but that fat, veiny cock. Make it feel good. Worship it. He withdraws again, then plunges deep. This time I'm ready for him: I let my throat gape wide.

He drives home with a fury that catches me off guard. My nose twists sideways under the weight of him, the nostrils full of his pubes and compressed by brute force. He shoves my head so deeply into the pillow that it wraps around my ears, cutting off all sound. For long moments, I'm deaf, speechless, and blind. Cut off from the world, thanks to his dick.

Panic urges me to slap the mattress, to buck him off me, but I don't want this moment to end. Oscar's rod is all I need. I'll do anything in this moment to make him feel good.

Reality rushes back when he withdraws once more, and my head surfaces from below the pillows. He gives me a moment to choke air into my lungs. I gasp and blink to clear my bleary eyes and find him looking down at me with something like condescension. "Cocksucker," he whispers. I can't help but moan from the way he mingles derision with fondness. "You love this big dick."

The object in question projects toward me, right before my eyes. The scent of hot flesh basted in saliva makes me hungrier. Furiously I nod, hoping he'll feed me more.

Instead, he rubs the apple-like head on my lips, spreading his salty pre-cum like balm. No matter how much with my eyes I plead, he refuses to let me do more than lick at it. "Million-dollar mouth," Oscar whispers while his dick slaps across my cheekbones, wet and heavy. "I can see how a man gets a sample of that kisser then wants to lock it away in some deee-luxe apartment." He shoves his thumb between my lips. Immediately, I apply suction and swirl my tongue around it, sucking it like dick. "That's exactly what I mean, Daddy. Million-dollar mouth."

"More," I beg, panting heavily. The feral in me is emerging.

Oscar withdraws his thumb, then applies my moisture to his nipple before he pinches himself. "Open." I obey. Slowly, too slowly, he begins to sink himself into my soft, wet offering. He's in no hurry to satisfy my hunger. If anything, he taunts me by refusing its entire length. I can't lunge forward to gulp it down, either; he's stretched his fingers around my neck to keep me still. "That's it. Get it slick." An inch more, before he pulls out and slides in again. "Get your boy good and wet."

His talk drives me crazy. My untouched cock leaps and strains with every word. Every time he withdraws, I spy the shine I'm leaving on his skin. When he pulls out altogether, big, ropy strands of my drool tether me to his dick's head.

With a cupped hand, he scoops up those slimy tendrils and slaps them upon his meat. "I can't stand it anymore."

He's made a decision. There's tightness around my ankles as, without warning, he yanks my legs upward; before I can fully comprehend that I've landed flat on my back, he's on top of me, slavering like a wild dog. Exquisite pain sears my right nipple as he chomps down. Again, on my left. I can feel the scarlet traces across my pale skin that his beard leaves as he rakes his chin across my torso. I'll be able to see them myself later, when eventually I clean myself up in the shower. Or perhaps for days later, every time I look down. For now, I am satisfied to know I bear his mark.

Now, Oscar grabs pillow after pillow and arranges them in a pile. Like I weigh nothing, he flips me atop them with my hips at the apex. "You want that ass fucked, daddy?"

"Yes." My whimper isn't enough for him. I almost

hear the sharp slap before I feel the impact and heat of his hand on my meaty butt. "*Yes!*" I yell, filling the room with sound.

"Again." Another smack, this time on my other cheek.

"Yes sir!" This bedroom has never had its hush so thoroughly shattered.

"Again!"

He batters my cheeks until they prickle with blood and fire. I'm confused by the noises I make. There's pain and outrage and tears as he assaults me with every deliberate wallop...and laughter, too? Yes, laughter, bubbling under every gasp and groan. How it has ached for release.

The fact is: I've never been so happy in my life. Ass up, pucker exposed, I don't need to pretend culture, or smarts, or sophistication. Oscar is affording me freedom from those shackles. He's allowing me to be nothing but hole. His hole. It's the finest gift I've ever received.

"Buckle up." The gardener seizes first one wrist, then the other. At the small of my back, he clutches them both with a single hand. I hear him spit, then add his moisture to mine on his dick. "You ready for your boy, daddy?"

My laughter surfaces once more, this time compounded with anticipation. I utter a soft supplication. "Make it hurt. Please, make it hurt. Make it...*fuu-uuuuuck.*"

Whether he's heard it or not, Oscar answers my prayer with a thrust, forcing open a hole that hasn't been plundered in three decades. Okay, technically untrue. In recent months, I'd bought toys for myself, now that I don't have to hide them. Clammy silicone doesn't begin to compare with warm, silky-slick flesh, though— and none of my dildos are as thick as the bull cock digging out my guts.

His onslaught hurts, all right. But even through the

pain wracks my body and causes my toes to curl, it's right. My distress is necessary. After too long a slumber, I'm awakening again. Feeling things.

Even agony seems good.

"Fuck me," I beg. "Please, fuck me. Open me up."

He's in, now. All of him. If his entire weight weren't on me, I might try to squirm away from the torment of his thick base stretching my hole past its limits. Instead, I have no choice but to accept as he grinds insistently into the muscles of my ass. His dick's blunt head nudges, then bludgeons that sweet button of my prostate, sending shivery pleasures reverberating along my spine.

Oh, I pretend I have no options—but I'm a willing collaborator in the destruction of my hole. Back I push against him, struggling to admit his every agonizing millimeter. He senses my need and mutters to himself, spitting in the crevice where cock meets hole to make himself even more slippery.

"Wreck me," I urge.

When he frees my wrists and props himself against the headboard, my forearms curl around the pillows. I press my face deep into their cool depths and arch my back. "That's right, daddy," Oscar purrs. "Get that pussy good and open for your boy."

Seems my boy is doing a thorough job of that, all by himself. Every determined thrust batters my resistance until only shreds remain. Soon, they follow, reduced to smithereens by the sheer force of his stabs. I pant like a bitch in heat. My hips rise higher, wider. All I want for my hole is more sensation, more pleasure, more pain.

"God *damn* it, Johnny." Somehow, I've pissed off Oscar. I can hear it in his changed tone. Yet frankly, I don't give a damn, so long as he keeps savaging my hole. "I told myself I wasn't going to do this." Before I can claw my thinking mind back from the brink, he pins down my skull with the base of his hand and growls in my ear. "I told myself that you're too classy a guy to treat like a slut, that I was gonna be real sweet all night, make it nice for you." His words take on a snarling edge. "But you *make...me...do...this.*"

He accompanies each of the last four words with a brutal drive of his hips. Four short times I cry out in loud lamentation—but not complaint. Never complaint. If I'd thought the wide base of his weapon dangerous before, I am unprepared for its temper-fueled lethality.

His monologue continues, punctuated with heavy breathing. "You make me treat you like a cheap little cocksucker." I nod with vigor. That's what I am. A cheap little cocksucker. "You *make* me fuck you like you're my personal faggot." Yes. Yes! I tremble at that thought. "You fuckin' make me lose my cool, so all I want is to bust my nut in this ass."

"Do it. Please." I am not too proud to beg.

"That what you want?" It truly is a good thing Helga lives elsewhere, because his voice is loud and insistent enough to carry to the far greenhouse. "My nut in your butt?"

I crane to look him in the face. Over my shoulder, all that's really visible is a curtain of dark, shining hair hanging down. "Breed me. Please. I need my boy's seed inside."

"Shit. You're doing it again." With a hand, he swipes the hair from his face so that I get a glimpse of those brown eyes. "Fuckin' cock whore. Nasty dick hog." Epithets worse than those tumble from his lips as I strain to maintain my link with his glazed and dilated eyes.

A fucking from Oscar is like ordering Thai food with extra chilis: absolute agony followed by transformation, as the heat and pain render the meal's every subtlety in stark relief. With every nerve aflame, I feel everything. His ample foreskin as it glides in my chute. The exposed ridge of his cock head as he ruins me. The smallest droplets of his spittle as the slurs continue to fly. I can hear the gentle click of the blinds above the bed, distinguish the thread count of my sheets upon my chest. On my ass and shoulders, where his hands squeeze and clutch, I enumerate every ridge and whorl imprinted upon his fingertips.

"Faggot," he spits again. "Whore. Sleazy piece of ass." I'd bristle at these words on the street, but here, in this space, I know they're spoken as praise. The whispered insults cascading from his mouth are what carry him forward upon his wave of pleasure; they're a litany of gratitude couched in profanities. Here, now, in this moment, I am proud to be his sleazy piece of ass.

"Do it," I urge. I can tell from his wild rabbiting that he's close. "Breed your whore. Daddy needs it."

He croaks out the words, "Yeah, daddy. Fuck! Look what you're making me...!" I yell and nosedive into the pillows as his meat swells and plunges deep. His roar shakes the earth. Oscar thunders as if racked with pain as he unloads a bucket of hot seed deep inside me. My hips rise to meet him; I squeeze my pelvic floor to milk every ounce of that precious fluid. More importantly, I clamp down to keep him from getting away. "Shit!" he yells, thrashing one last time.

Our exertion has left us covered in sweat. My pelvis still uncomfortably high, I squeeze and grind while he mutters curses and wipes perspiration from his face. After a moment in which neither of us moves, I feel him stir behind me. "Don't pull out," I plead.

"I'm not." He presses at the base of my spine, pushing me into the nest of pillows. His cock still buried, he settles atop me. For a moment, I feel his full weight and the warmth of his chest; I adjust as he surrounds me with strong arms.

Together we roll onto our left sides. Oscar releases a deep sigh—contented, I like to think—in the vicinity of my ear. Every hair inside stirs and tickles. Our repose only lasts a moment, until he lifts his uppermost hand to his mouth, spits in his paw, and curls the sloppy mess around my cock. "No," I say, alarmed. "You don't have to."

"Shush, now." His hips slowly grind into my butt. He's still three-quarters hard. "I want to." I must admit that his hand feels good. My dick's nowhere his size, but he plays me like a master musician might his instrument. "Just enjoy."

His lips toy with my ear, kiss my shoulder, pepper the back of my neck with the softest of pressure. Meanwhile, his inked left arm curls around my body. That hand tugs and teases at my nipple, while the other continues to slide rapidly up and down my shaft. I can't help but give in. This may be the first time a man had held me and insisted I savor his attention.

"When's the last time anyone really saw you, baby?" he murmurs, reading my mind again. "Saw you as a man with needs of his own?"

I know the answer. But because replying would bring me shame, I shrug and let him manipulate my sensitive shaft.

"That's okay. Because nah. I'm not going to pop my load and forget about my daddy." He accompanies the promise with a sloppy thrust of his cock, using his own seed to nuzzle his snout deeper inside. I harden further and stir like a cat awakened. "It's okay, baby," he whispers, picking up the pace. My breathing intensifies. "Give me that daddy load."

With his encouragement, I push backward onto his still-swollen meat and allow him to guide me over the edge.

Over the decades, here in my own home, I've always had to conceal my masturbation. From habit, tonight I climax with little more than the gentlest of sighs, the merest exclamation of pleasure. Semen shoots from my cock all over the sheets, but because his cock still presses against the fiery knob of my prostate, it's there my pleasure finds a center. I clamp down on his meat and allow my stretched and tortured flesh to convulse while my body shudders and shakes. For years, my hole has been too empty. Only now can I say I have been properly filled.

For who knows how long, the two of us have formed the axis of the world; everything has revolved around our coupling. Now, as we relax, the city outside begins to trickle in. The sound of traffic, the distant noise of sirens, the blare of a pedicab's overloud speakers on the nighttime streets. The tick of the ancient electric clock on Kenneth's side of the bed. Oscar breathes deeply, but he makes no attempt to move. I hope he won't. Not for a while.

"The spreadsheet you gave me," I venture.

"Mmm?" Oscar chuckles a little from beneath the blanket of slumber that descends on us both, as if I've resurrected a funny memory from years ago. "What about it?"

"Thank you for all that work. But come back and teach me." His arm around my ribcage, fingers still sticky with my load, pulls me closer. "Show me how to use those gadgets. Teach me how to bring those orchids to life again." The rumble in his chest as he settles in reassures me. "I don't think it's too late to learn."

"Oh, Johnny." Oscar plants a soft kiss on my nape that leaves me shivering. He's mere moments away from falling asleep. "I knew I'd make a gardener out of you."

His hand trails from my chest to my belly, at last coming to rest at the cleft in my legs. Upon those warm ridges raised by his touch, flowers seem to blossom.

Acknowledgments

I am indebted to my friends Al and Michael Jay for their contributions to this story of a late-in-life flowering. I commend the former for his late-draft sharp comments that helped bring elements into focus; the latter, with an endless supply of good humor, suggested what a protagonist much more fashionable than I might wear for the story's scenarios.

To these fine gentlemen, I dedicate this steamy slice of smut.

About the Authors

Peter Schutes is the nom de plume of a prolific and acclaimed novelist. As Peter Schutes, he is the author of Adult Erotic Fiction such as <u>The Slaves of Rome</u>, <u>Dark as a Dungeon</u>, <u>The Gospel of Priapus</u>, and <u>Panama Heat</u>. He writes in the style of vintage pulp authors from the 1960s and 1970s. He lives in Los Angeles.

Chuck Idgaf is a relatively new queer author. Deep into middle age, Chuck decided to broaden his hobbies, writing very erotic short stories. Initially, he just shared them with friends. The collaboration with Jim Dandy is the first time his work will be widely available. Chuck has a fondness for bears and daddies, so those tend to be common themes. He also likes stories about coming out, first times, and exploring new experiences. If you can't figure it out from the dialogue in his stories, Chuck grew up in the Deep South. He now lives in the Coachella Valley, California, with his husband.

J. W. Steed is pleased to be making his pseudonymous debut in this anthology. He is the author of more than a dozen mainstream novels and also writes memoir and humorous essays. He teaches creative writing in the metro NYC area and is active in the Science Fiction and Fantasy Writer's Association (SFWA).

Also from Peter Schutes Publishing

Please visit Peter's Website to find links to all of Peter's books.

PAPERBACKS

Big Bodies of All Sizes

Big Hole River

Bobbing Buoys and Salty Seamen

Confessions of a Rodeo Clown

Cosmic Cage: Gay SF Erotica

Dirty Dorms and Fresh Men

Filthy Jobs and Steamy Showers

The Gospel of Priapus

Hoboes, Hustlers, and Outlaws

Hot Blue Collars

Like the Greeks Do

Muscle Bottom

Same Sex: Gay SF Clone Erotica

Satanic Seductions

The Slaves of Rome

Small Cockpits and Big Hangars

Tales of Two Daddies

E-BOOKS

The Able Seaman

The Anaconda Copper

The Artist

The Autobiography of Peter Schutes

Backwoods Delivery

Billy Club

Buck Private

Bunkhouse Buddies

The Butt Baby

Chopper Jock

Cloistered

Coached

Dark as a Dungeon

Demonic Deception *aka* Deceived, Cursed & Blessed

Desert Island Daddies

Dutch Treat

Edging the Lawn

The Expectant Member

Firehouse Lovers

The Fish

Five Erotic Tales

Hercules and Lippos

Hobo Honey

Hotshot

Little Shamus

Logger's Delight

On the Block

Panama Heat

Satan's Sissy Boy

The Spotter

Steroid Steve

The Thigh Baby

Under the Boardwalk

Wee Dobbin

World's Biggest

***** Coming Soon *****

PAPERBACKS

Tales of Two More Daddies

Highways and Bi-ways: GAy SF On the Road

E-BOOKS

The Artist

Billy Club

The City Gardener

Edging the Lawn

The Good Dad

In Each Other's Arms

Lift Pump

The Longshoremen

The Most Dangerous Flower

The Orchardman

Poolside Plantings

Slapjack

Tuxes n' Tails

About Mowing and Blowing

FOUR STORIES ALL ABOUT TRIMMING, MOWING, PRUNING, EDGING, AND BLOWING.

The City Gardener: I'm Pedro, but I go by Pete. I have a really big problem, and it isn't just my drinking. When my struggle becomes too much, a stranger helps me out in all the right ways.

Edging the Lawn: I came up with a cool way to earn some cash in the summer before college. A hot daddy hires me to mow his lawn, and then gives me a huge tip!

Poolside Plantings: On hiatus from the movie biz, Palm Springs is just the place to relax and watch the garden grow into full bloom.

The Most Dangerous Flower: Recently widowed, I don't know a thing about caring for my late lover's orchids. Oscar does. He shows me the ropes and waters things just right.